aly

PRAISE FOR **THE GAME WE PLAY**

"Susan Hope Lanier's collection of brilliant short stories, *The Game We Play*, is a triumph. Detailing distinct
human relationships, moments of connection, and
modern crises, these stories—all effortlessly rendered,
all deeply felt—evoke the best of Raymond Carver and
Lorrie Moore. An outstanding debut that should reaf-
firm our shared belief in the absolute necessity and
imaginative possibility of the short story."

—JOE MENO, author of *The Great Perhaps* and
Hairstyles of the Damned

"There's such pathos, humor, and sadness in the stories
in Susan Hope Lanier's collection, *The Game We Play*,
that I sometimes found myself holding my breath as I
turned the pages. Lanier's characters, with their heartbreak and joys, their frustrations and fears, will stay in
your thoughts long after you read the final sentence of
this accomplished first book."

—CHRISTINE SNEED, author of *Little Known Facts* and
Portraits of a Few of the P

"Lanier's deceptively breezy prose may pour off the page as easily as water flows from the tap, but her unassuming way with words actually requires great finesse. Apparently fluent in the unvarnished dialect we speak in our own thoughts, Lanier adroitly avoids the trap of trying too hard to sound clever. Instead, she relies on cutting wit, keen powers of observation, and an easily swollen heart to shine light on awkward truths in a way that renders them almost deliciously painful. Without glamorizing youthful malaise, her flawed but endearing characters bump—and sometimes grind—against each other, leaving the kinds of bruises that turn into lingering regret and inconvenient wisdom. In *The Game We Play*, Lanier manages to be understated and unflinching at the same time and strides forward with a confident, highly compassionate debut."

—SABY REYES-KULKARNI, *Paste*

THE GAME WE PLAY

STORIES

SUSAN HOPE LANIER

CURBSIDE SPLENDOR PUBLISHING

The stories contained herein are works of fiction. All incidents, situations, institutions, governments, and people are fictional and any similarity to characters or persons living or dead is strictly coincidental.

Published by Curbside Splendor Publishing, Inc., Chicago, Illinois in 2014.

First Edition
Copyright © 2014 by Susan Hope Lanier
Library of Congress Control Number: 2014945066

ISBN 978-1-940430-27-0
Edited by Peter Jurmu
Cover photograph by Nick Marshall
Designed by Alban Fischer

Manufactured in the United States of America.

www.curbsidesplendor.com

FOR JD AND JF

CONTENTS

HOW TOMMY SOTO BREAKS YOUR HEART

1

Tommy Soto is short and it is embarrassing. He is both Mexican and Jewish, and that is peculiar. He is freckled and in drama club. He has braces but still eats popcorn. All of it makes you feel so very sorry for him. This is how Tommy Soto breaks your heart.

2

When the towers fall you obsessively watch the news in first and second period and hope the death toll rises. People will care more, you justify, and it will become a bigger tragedy. You think everyone will feel important again. The only person you tell about your silent wish is Tommy Soto, and when you do he says, "You're terrible."

That is how your heart feels. Terrible.

3

The morning after you get back from Mexico, where your brother married a Colombian girl who was only 5′2″ even in three-inch heels, your mother says to you, "Darling, you should really consider dating that Tommy boy next door."

She prides herself on being open-minded *and* a lobbyist for free trade.

You are in the kitchen and Mom is cutting seedless grapes in half for a Waldorf salad on a wooden cutting board. "You know," she says, "add even more diversity to this family."

This is why everyone hates America.

This is why Tommy Soto hates your mom.

This is why you have a faulty heart.

4

Everyone at school calls Tommy MexiJew, and you have yet to tell your friends that you've been fucking him in your car after school for the last two months. You resent your mom for making you drive to school in an apple-red minivan with a Star Trek bumper sticker and vanity plates that say *BE ME UP*. You resent your friends for calling Tommy "faggot" because you have two months' worth of proof to the contrary. And you are actually, secretly, very much in love with him.

Still, the way you say "no" when he asks you if you'd like to go to the mall sometime makes you feel like you have the tiniest heart.

5

After spending all morning staring at the news, you and Tommy eat lunch behind the overflow trailers where no one can see you. He eats your packed lunch. You eat his bought lunch off a pink Styrofoam tray.

"You know, there's another plane and they say it's headed for the Capitol building. They say it's going right for your mom."

Even though you hate your Mom, maybe even more than Tommy hates your mom, you are hurt.

"Why would you say that?" you ask. Only you have permission to say such awful things.

"Because it's true."

Tommy pops one of your mom's grapes into his mouth and you swear he is eating your heart.

6

Later you can see a popcorn kernel in Tommy's crooked teeth when he holds out a can of Coke and smiles. He bought this soda just for you. It's his version of an apology. The whole school is convening on the football bleachers to talk about everyone's feelings.

Justine O'Donald—the little bitch, you hate her fake blond hair and perfect shoes—passes Tommy on the bleacher stairs and sits directly behind you. She leans in and loudly whispers, "I feel like if you fuck a terrorist, then you are a terrorist."

You wave the Coke can away from your face. You even say, "Get lost," and Justine laughs.

Tommy doesn't say anything. A desperation in his dark brown eyes trickles down to his outstretched hand. You look at the can of Coke, then back to his pudgy, freckled face, and you shrug. It is the smallest shrug ever. An ant could not shrug a shrug as small. You must make it into the Guinness Book of World Records with a shrug like this, and still, somehow, even though it is just the tiniest thing ever, you know Tommy knows you feel bad. You are sorry. It's just that Justine is laughing her perfect hyena laugh, and she is totally pulverizing your heart.

7

Ten minutes later, a half-empty Coke can hits you in the back of the head. You feel the liquid run to the tips of your split ends and down your neck, and you know almost instantly who threw it. You don't want to touch your throbbing skull or wipe the tears out of your eyes. You don't even want to look in his direction. You don't want to give him the satisfaction. You just stare down into your lap and hope no one sees you crying, and if they do, at the very least your mascara isn't running.

But you can't do it. You have to look. You crane your head back and to the left.

The whole school is staring at you. Everyone but Tommy. He isn't even vaguely looking in your direction. He high-fives someone you do not know. Someone else grabs him around the neck and gives him a brotherly shake. He is all laughter and smiles and good times. You've never seen his freckled face look this happy and you know all those other times were just practice for this. Your heart is broken.

CAT AND BIRD

Alice looked like she listened to bands with names like Bad Skulls, or Fuck Mullet or Kill Whatever Whatever, all things Chloe knew exactly nothing about. She had a pizza tattoo on her right forearm and a dark '80s shag haircut. She looked so cool in her skintight jeans, Asics, and *Beavis and Butthead* t-shirt. The moment she lit a cigarette in the quad—a definite no-smoking zone in the brickshit city that was their new college campus in Rochester, New York—Chloe knew she wanted to be friends with her.

It was the fall of '00, Chloe's first week of college, and everywhere she turned, someone had blank voter registration cards.

"You know, you can't smoke out here," some tall goof said while trying to hand Alice his pen and clipboard. Alice took a drag of her cigarette, placing it right in the middle of her lips with her fingers choked up almost past the filter, and exhaled in his face.

"Get lost," Alice said. And he did.

Even though Chloe could feel the hard plastic of her lighter digging against her hip in the pocket of her blue jeans, she asked Alice to bum a light.

"You're really beautiful," Alice said, passing the matchbook.

Chloe couldn't help but blush. She felt like a piece of paper—plain, boring, flimsy—and truly believed she had no unusual, distinguishing features, nothing about her that one could remember in her absence aside from her 2% milk skin. One might notice her unplucked eyebrows, that she didn't even wear makeup, that she had a small pink birthmark under her chin, that the left nostril of her otherwise perfect upturned nose was ever so slightly larger than the right one. Chloe ordinarily did not dwell on these imperfections. Sure, she would agonize over her clothes, whether to wear glasses or contacts, how to style her unruly curly hair, but underneath all that she knew she was perceived as being vaguely attractive. Enough makeouts in high school had said as much. Still, hearing it from Alice was another thing entirely. None of her friends back home ever complimented each other so openly, and if they did, they would never, ever use the word "beautiful." Things were pretty or ugly, cool or lame, but never beautiful. That adjective's use was reserved solely for mothers fawning over their daughters' prom dresses. But out of Alice's mouth, it sounded sophisticated in a way that Midwestern mothers never were.

If Chloe had decided she wanted to be anything in college, it was sophisticated. She wanted to be one of those girls who could use the word "woman" to describe her peers without sounding pretentious. Was Alice a woman? It still sounded entirely too awkward.

That Chloe considered Alice one of the prettiest, coolest girls she had ever met only fed her embarrassment as her cheeks tensed into a bright red smile. No, no, no, she hadn't wanted Alice to see how much pleasure the compliment had given her, but so much for that. She had already smiled like a damn fool. She worried Alice would misunderstand this as a constant need for reassurance, when really she felt intense satisfaction from impressing people. That needing reassurance and wanting to impress people are different sides of the same coin did not occur to her.

"Thanks, I guess," Chloe said, folding back the matchbook's face and striking a light. The flame went out.

"I mean it." Alice took the matches. She cupped a hand around the end of Chloe's cigarette and struck another light. "You are. I don't know why you have to be all insecure about it," she said, the cigarette between her lips bouncing up and down when she spoke.

"I'm not."

"Oh, I'm just kidding, Birdy," Alice said.

Birdy. It flicked off Alice's tongue like she was blowing bubble gum. Chloe later learned Alice reserved the nickname for her closest friends. Birdy. The sweet sound of it, while strangely endearing, seemed false. By the third week of classes, Alice had recounted what Chloe assumed was her entire life story and so Chloe had decided that the intimacy she heard in the nickname was just a remnant from Alice's childhood.

Alice was born in Niagara Falls. Her mom wrote for *The Democrat and Chronicle* and lived in Albany. Her dad was a hotshot lawyer who had moved on to wife number five. Alice could not stand either of them. Her dad phoned almost daily, and every time Alice answered his calls she rolled her big brown eyes.

Chloe could only imagine. Her parents were still happily married. He was a postal worker, she was a nurse. Still, Chloe couldn't help but feel like Alice was giving her parents a bad rap. Even though she was a first-year, she had managed to score a single room in the dorms. The walls of the eight-by-ten box were lined with Christmas lights and framed posters of the Smiths and the Misfits, her favorite bands. She had a matching hot pink iMac and stereo on her desk, and at least a hundred CDs hanging in a metal rack on the back of her door. The first time Chloe had seen Alice's room she said "Wow" like a total dork.

Alice shrugged it off. "Oh, the parentals didn't know how else to say goodbye. So they did what they always do." She rubbed her thumb and index finger together.

Chloe didn't say anything to that. The way her own parents said goodbye hadn't been much better.

Don't feel like you have to call home. Those were the words Chloe's mom had said when hugging her daughter goodbye at O'Hare. Mom let go just as the intercom buzzed that the flight to Rochester was now boarding. Handing Chloe the rolling suitcase's handle, Mom also said, "Bad news travels fast enough."

Looking into her mother's blue eyes, Chloe thought she understood that her mom wasn't worried about her. She would do just fine. Chloe rocked forward, up onto her toes to hug her father, a bear of a man with long arms and a small beer belly. He whispered, "Call whenever you like."

After she lined up at the gate, she heard her parents arguing. "What the hell was that? What kind of a thing is that to say to our daughter when she leaves for college?" her father said, the words fading into the din of the airport as they walked away, her mother three or four strides in front of him. It wasn't until Chloe shoved her suitcase in the overhead compartment and clicked in her seatbelt, that her eyes began to sting. *Dad was right. Don't feel like you need to call home? Bad news travels fast enough? What the hell did that mean anyway?*

Chloe wanted off the stupid plane. She imagined grabbing her suitcase and pushing the passengers that were still trying to find their seats out of the way. Running through the massive gray terminal and seeing the dark curls of her mother's hair bobbing in the distance. She imagined reaching her just before the security check and putting a hand on her shoulder. What Chloe could not figure out was what she would say when her mother turned around. She didn't know, so she stayed strapped into her window seat over the plane's left wing.

When Alice brushed her parents off by flashing the sign for money Chloe realized she probably would never have the guts to confront her own mom. Chloe envied Alice. She envied her ability to hate her parents so completely that she could casually dismiss them with a simple gesture.

By early October, Chloe had put a blonde streak in her hair, gauged her ears and bought her first pair of blue-black Doc Martens. The campus was buzzing about the upcoming national elections. Alice couldn't care less.

"No way is Gore losing. Bush is a total idiot. And besides, politicians are evil. I don't think I'm even going to vote. It's not like it changes anything anyway," Alice said, trailing her black nails along the VHS cases in the comedy section.

They were cruising the local Blockbuster, looking for costume ideas even though Halloween was more than three weeks away. They planned to dress as a pair. A lame romance with Julia Roberts played on small television screens that hung from the ceiling.

"I think you should vote," Chloe said. She was thoroughly annoyed that the pimple-faced girl behind the cash register at the front of the store didn't think maybe it would be a good idea to put it on CNN or something. Chloe was annoyed that she was here, period. She wanted to be back in her room watching the second presidential debate.

"Oh, you do?" Alice said.

"Well yeah. It's like, a duty."

Alice shrugged, "I'm not registered anyway."

"You still can," Chloe said. She was sure Alice's lack of interest in politics had something to do with her parents.

"I don't want to talk about it, okay? No offense or anything."

No, Alice was only concerned about Halloween and that both of them had perfect costumes. She had said she wanted to go for something early-Nineties ironic, but Chloe had no idea what that even meant and suspected Alice didn't either. It just sounded cool.

Chloe held up a copy of *Ghostbusters*.

"I don't know," Alice said. "Is one of us supposed to be Bill Murray, and the other, like, a ghost monster?"

"Sure, and we could do it real hokey. Like, you just wear a sheet with two eye holes."

"Oh, so I get to be the ghost? No offense or anything, but I am not wearing a lame sheet as my Halloween costume."

"Or, I could be the ghost. I really don't—"

"Oh my god," Alice interrupted, pulling a VHS tape off the shelf. "*Wayne's World*!" She held up the tape like a model on *The Price Is Right*, her right hand waving below the caption. *You'll laugh. You'll cry. You'll hurl.*

"What about it?"

"Birdy, it's perfect."

"I've never seen it."

Watching *Wayne's World* was a rite of passage, but Chloe had just never gotten around to watching it, like how she hadn't gotten around to listening to the punk mixtape Alice had made for her.

"Are you serious? It's like, only the best movie. We have to watch it immediately."

Chloe wasn't sure why she agreed to it. She didn't want to watch some stupid movie. She didn't want to sit in a hard desk chair while Alice sprawled out on her bed, got high, ate popcorn and fell asleep before the movie even ended. But something about Alice made her impossible to refuse. She didn't seem to care about anything, and look at her: she was happy all of the time. Not that Chloe was miserable, but she still thought that maybe it was time to take a little time away from the land of the caring.

"I just know you're going to love it," Alice said, popping *Wayne's World* into the VCR slot of her TV combo. She had changed into a pair of black pajama pants and a sweatshirt. Chloe sat cross-legged on the wooden chair she had moved around the side of the bed.

"You know you can lay with me, right?" Alice said. She pulled back her lime green comforter. Chloe slipped off her boots and crawled into bed. Alice rested her head on Chloe's shoulder, and they watched like this, snuggled up together, passing a bowl and blowing the smoke through a cardboard toilet paper roll stuffed with dryer sheets. At first Alice's body next to her felt awkward, but as the weed hit, Chloe settled into her. She could not stop laughing and eating popcorn. By the time Alice Cooper appeared in the movie, Chloe was so high she couldn't feel her face.

Alice Cooper was shirtless with two streaks of black makeup running down his cheeks. Wayne and Garth knelt at his feet, bowing to him, "We're not worthy, we're not worthy!" Chloe turned to the Alice lying beside her and waved her hands up and down, bowing and saying, "We're not worthy, we're not worthy!" Alice and Chloe laughed wildly, until the popcorn bowl, empty except for the hard, brown kernels slid off the bed and onto the floor.

When they calmed down and caught their breath, Alice hugged Chloe. She smelled bittersweet, like grapefruit and stale coffee.

"Meow meow meow," Alice whispered into her ear.

It felt like a secret. In that moment Chloe knew that Alice's tough-as-nails attitude was really just a front. For the first time she felt like she could say anything, do anything, with Alice.

"I love you so much," Chloe said. She could hardly believe the words coming out of her mouth.

"I love you too, Birdy," Alice said.

Chloe was pretty sure she meant it.

Chloe hadn't thought of her parents since the first week of school, but the moment she heard her father's voice saying "Hey Clo," she missed them.

Her dad had always been the happy one in the family. As a kid, she loved the way he would pick her up before bedtime. He'd drape her legs over each forearm, one on each side, with her bottom dangling in the middle. Then he would stick up his thumbs, and Chloe would hold onto them and use them like joysticks as he made helicopter noises with his tongue. She'd steer them to her bed.

"What's up, Dad?" The way he had said her name sounded strange, the "o" in Clo falling like a heavy brick.

"Just saying hi. Miss you."

"Miss you too. Is Mom around?"

Her dad didn't respond, and words hung lost in telephone lines between Illinois and New York. "Dad?"

"She's not here." Another pause. "But I'm sure she misses you."

"Is everything okay, dad?"

"Of course," he said. Then, "Don't be a stranger."

"I wont."

"Love you." The phone clicked. He didn't wait for Chloe to say it back.

That night in bed Chloe played the whole fifty-second conversation over in her head. *I'm sure she misses you.* It sounded like a guess. Chloe imagined her parents wandering through their small ranch house, passing one another in silence.

The day after the last presidential debate, Students For Gore set up a table in Gracie's, the dining hall reserved for the sole use of the freshman class. The table was in front of the floor-to-ceiling windows at the far end of the cafeteria. A kid wearing an oversized flannel sat behind the SFG table reading a book. Chloe could just make out his thick clear-framed glasses from her seat by the exit. In the twenty minutes Chloe took to eat her lunch, not a single student approached the table, so she decided to.

"No one is interested, huh?" she said.

He looked up from his book. Faint freckles dotted his

high cheekbones. Chloe was running late to English 101, but fuck it. He was just too adorable.

"No one cares," he said. "They should, but they don't."

"Did you watch the debate?"

"Sure. Bush sounded like an idiot. Same old Republican bullshit. Money for the rich."

A pair of arms wrapped around Chloe's middle.

"Birdy!" Chloe saw the black nail polish on the end of Alice's fingers. "Guess what."

Chloe turned around.

"I found the perfect Halloween party. It's at those industrial loft spaces on East Main." She handed her a flyer. *Boo!* was written in white block letters on a black background.

Then she did it. That thing. She said, "Meow, meow, meow."

In the past few weeks it had become a regular term of endearment. Sometimes Alice even pawed, or kneaded her like a kitten, but she had never done it in public.

Chloe blushed. No, no, no. It was their thing, to say behind closed doors, not with cute guys watching. He rolled his eyes. Great. Now he thought she was an idiot, like she was Alice's pet or something.

Alice leaned over the table, her feet still barely on the tiled floor. "Come if you wanna," she said sliding a folded flyer into the pocket of his flannel. Then she pursed her lips and said, "Trust me, you wanna."

His eyes grew wide, and his mouth turned into an O, and that's when Chloe knew she no longer had a chance. Alice spent the rest of the week gushing about Specks. That was her nickname for him. Specks. She said he smelled like milk and looked like Cobain, except "Asian." She did not mention what Chloe thought were his best features: his adorable freckles and political inclinations.

The blonde Garth wig that Chloe had spent thirty dollars on was already making her scalp itch, but she tried to ignore it as the loud bass thumped through the graffiti-covered stairwell. They both looked pretty good. Alice had copied the *Wayne's World* logo really well with white fabric paint onto a black trucker hat, and Chloe had managed to find Garth's Aerosmith t-shirt after a diligent two-week search on eBay. They even had a black boombox with a cassette tape of the soundtrack. Still, Chloe didn't feel comfortable. She had wanted to dress up as Wayne.

"But you wear glasses already," Alice had said, and that ended the subject.

Alice had a point, but now Chloe worried that she looked like a total dork in the glasses she hadn't worn since ninth grade. Alice looked as pretty as ever. Her costume was simple and she had the ability to still look sexy even in a t-shirt and jeans. It helped that she wore bright red lipstick. When Chloe brought up the fact that she felt like she was pulling most of the weight, that she looked more dressed up and stupid, like she was trying too hard, Alice rolled her eyes. "You look great," she said.

Alice turned to the hard, wooden door and pounded three times with the pinky side of her fist. Then she licked the tips of her fingers and tucked a loose strand of Chloe's brown hair back under the blond wig. "Don't be so insecure, okay?" Alice put her hands on both of Chloe's shoulders and squeezed. "We look totally awesome."

Chloe shrugged.

Alice hugged her, and whispered "Meow, meow, meow" into her left ear just as the door swung open.

What once felt like a secret now felt like a leash.

They both looked up at a tall, lanky guy who was dressed in black leather as Eric from *The Crow*. His face was caked in thick layers of white and black makeup. Construction paper bats hung from the ceiling behind him.

"Ha, ha, niiiiiice," Eric said with a smile. His teeth looked perfectly white against his black lipstick. "I love that movie."

"See, I told you so," Alice said pushing Chloe through the doorway. "Everyone will love it."

By midnight, Alice was nowhere to be seen and Chloe had drunk four beers. She sat on a grody paisley sofa with the black boom box in her lap. The Crow was sitting next to her entirely too close for comfort. She couldn't blame him really. *Midnite Vultures* was playing from the stereo and the party was so packed and loud that they had to scream inches away from each other's ears just to hear one another. Still, this guy, "Eric," was boring. He smelled like ketchup and would not stop talking about English 101.

"It's my favorite class."

"Really?" Everyone hated English 101. It was a total chore.

"I liked what you said about Gatsby last week."

"What?" Chloe yelled over the music.

"About Gatsby. How he resorts to crime just to make money to impress people. How like, totally shallow that is."

"Oh right," Chloe said. She looked at the Crow sideways. In profile his nose was a scalene triangle. Chloe was sure she had never seen him before and she couldn't believe Alice had left her with him.

"Your friend is kind of a bitch, huh?"

"What?"

"Your friend. She's kind of a bitch. She blew smoke in my face once."

"She's not a bitch. She's just opinionated," Chloe yelled, though on second thought, she wasn't so sure of Alice's opinions on anything except that The Smiths, Doc Martins, and *Wayne's World* were totally cool and that *Ghostbusters*, politics and English 101 were so totally not.

"What?" The Crow cupped his ear with his left hand.

"I'm going to get another beer."

He yelled something after her, but Chloe was already weaving through the crowd of smoke and bodies. She found Alice in the makeshift kitchen, sitting up on a wooden countertop next to a mini fridge, talking to some dude dressed as a ghost with a sheet over his head. It was much, much quieter in here, the sound of Beck a faint memory thumping against the walls.

"Birdy!" Alice yelled slipping off the counter to hug her with a half empty forty of Old English still in her hand. "Birdy this is Brody. Brody this is Chloe."

A long, thin hand appeared from under the sheet and pulled the ghost costume off. There he stood, the kid from Students for Gore.

"It's Specks," Alice said.

Brody put out his hand. "Nice to meet you, Chloe." His lips curled into a smile. It was dark in the kitchen so Chloe couldn't make out the faint freckles on his nose, but she knew they were there and couldn't help but smile back as she shook his hand.

"Isn't his costume great?" Alice said, putting an arm around Chloe's shoulder.

"Yeah. Really great. Ghost is just classic," Chloe said. She managed to keep her smile steady even though inside she was reeling. Alice would say anything, anything to make people like her, wouldn't she? Chloe knew Alice thought the costume was lame. Alice was totally full of shit.

Chloe slipped out of Alice's grasp by handing her the boom box before taking the forty out of her hand. Chloe had just decided she was going to get really fucking drunk. She pushed herself up onto the kitchen counter top, and took a huge swig of lukewarm malt.

"Actually, I was thinking of going as a ghost too," Chloe said.

"Yeah, but Garth and Wayne is definitely better."

"It was my idea," Alice said, taking all the credit. But look at her, she wasn't even authentic. Wayne didn't wear lipstick. She was just trying to be cute and it was embarrassing.

"Check this out." Chloe grabbed the boombox from Alice, placed it next to herself on the counter top and hit play. Freddie Mercury's voice hissed through the speakers. *Is this the real life? Is this just fantasy?* The ten or so people milling around the kitchen instantly turned into a chorus.

At the end of the first verse Chloe pushed herself up onto the countertop and pumped her fists in the air. Alice climbed on too, and the wood bowed in the middle. Halfway through, when the song breaks into unrelenting joy, Chloe felt her wig slip off, but she didn't care. The whole kitchen was now packed and everyone was looking up at them and singing along and it felt like a dream, like flying or floating or falling in love.

Chloe looked down at Brody who had disappeared under his ghost costume again. She could just make out the whites of his eyes through the holes in the sheet. They were on her. He wasn't looking at Alice, and his heels were pounding into the tiled floor. Chloe sang the rest of the song as if they were alone in a car. Right at the last line—everyone singing "Nothing really matters"—the countertop cracked and Chloe fell. Brody caught her and she stood there for a moment, the sheet a thin layer between her hands and his chest.

Fuck Alice. She pressed her lips against the thin, white sheet and felt Brody's lips kissing her back.

"Wow," Brody said when they parted, pulling the sheet off his head.

As the room erupted in cheers Chloe looked back behind her, up at the broken countertop, but Alice was gone.

An hour later she found Alice straddling Eric on the sofa, making out while the rest of the party buzzed on around them. Chloe tapped her on the shoulder and Alice turned around, rolled her eyes, and said, "What?"

"Can we talk about this?"

"What is there to talk about?" Alice dabbed her finger at the corner of her mouth and pulled back some of the makeup that was now smeared across her cheeks.

"Brody."

"Ew, Birdy. You can do better than that."

Chloe couldn't believe it. Alice had practically thrown

herself at Brody. *Oh your costume is so great. I just love it.* And now here she was sucking face with a total dweeb. Chloe crossed her arms and said, "Fuck you."

"Oh, lighten up, Birdy. Why do you have to be so serious all the time?" Alice put her hands around Eric's neck and his eyes turned into two white eggs.

"So what if I'm serious? It's better than not giving a fuck."

"Oh, elections are so cool. Oh, I'm going to go vote. Look at me vote. My name is Chloe and I am so cool because I care about politics and I kiss boys at parties."

"Well, at least *I'm* not all fake to get people to like me," Chloe said. "At least I don't have a million step-moms."

"What's that supposed to mean?"

"Isn't it obvious? It means you're the reason they left. It means no wonder your dad buys you off. It means he doesn't even want to be in the same room as you."

Chloe regretted it the second she said it.

Alice looked up at the ceiling and blinked twice. She inhaled deeply and mouthed "Whatever," then grabbed Eric by the hand and stormed from the party.

Chloe spent every meal after that at the Students for Gore table in Gracie's. She missed half a dozen classes and didn't turn in midterm papers. She handed out flyers to the few students who bothered to stop, and made eyes at Brody, who made eyes back.

Alice got all her meals to go, swinging a Styrofoam take-out box in a plastic bag past the table, without a word. Once, they both happened to find themselves at the soda fountain, going for the same paper cup. Alice crossed her arms—a steady silence between them, so thick Chloe could hear her own heart beating—before Alice turned and walked away, leaving her lunch on the silver countertop.

On Election Day, two networks had already called Florida for Gore when Chloe's phone rang.

"Hey Clo." It was her dad.

"What's up, Dad?"

"Are you coming home for Thanksgiving?" he said.

"Oh, I kind of just assumed—" Chloe flicked off the TV.

"Because maybe, if any of your friends are sticking around there—you know. Maybe you should stay," he said.

"Dad? What's going on?" Chloe prepared herself for a blow.

"I'm sorry Mom's not here to say hello. She's—" But he didn't need to finish his sentence.

"She's gone, isn't she?"

"I'm sorry, Clo."

"Okay."

"Talk soon?"

"Sure, Dad."

*

Chloe lit a cigarette in the quad, her hands shaking in the cold November air. The full weight of the previous night's phone conversation hit her at the same moment she saw Alice emerge from the building with Eric in tow. Alice and Chloe looked at each other in silence. Two streams of tears ran down Chloe's cheeks. She couldn't imagine going through this feeling more than once.

"I'm so sorry," Chloe said, wiping her tears with the cuff of her jack.

Alice lit her cigarette the way she always did, holding it just past the filter. "You know, it's still too close to call," Alice said, her used match falling to the ground between them.

"What?"

"The election. Your guy could still win it."

For just a moment Chloe thought she might be forgiven, but Alice turned to leave. Chloe wanted to reach out and stop her, to say the perfect thing, but she couldn't. There was nothing to say. As Alice walked down the long path to Gracie's, her shoulders hunched against the wind in a small leather jacket, Chloe whispered, "Yeah, he could still win it."

OVER SHELL DRIVE

Long before she knows her father's secrets, Sammy spills orange juice on her baby-doll dress hemmed by eyes of god.

Dad shakes his head and says, "Damn it." He makes a phone call to the elementary school, or to the office, or to Mom, who has already left for work.

Sammy changes into another dress—Dad's favorite, the blue one with the smocking and a big white bow around the waist. While he waits by the front door, Dad checks and rechecks his watch, though later he will admit to her that his heart swells with gratitude every time he remembers this delay.

When Sammy finally comes downstairs, his smile spreads the corners of his eyes into starburst.

"Help drive Bette today?" Dad asks.

"You're not mad?"

"I'm not mad," he says.

Bette is a warm-day-in-winter yellow. She always smells like McDonald's and stale cigarettes, but she's pretty. She feels the way home used to be.

This is the game they play: Dad tells Sammy to watch his left foot. The leather seat hums underneath her as the car gets louder, and right when Bette sounds like she'll fall apart Dad presses down on the clutch and yells a number.

Taking the corner on Shell Drive, Bette rattles so hard her yellow paint might flake off. "Two!" Dad says, and Sammy moves the stick from third to second. Bette flies over the hill. Sammy's thighs lift from the brown leather seat. As they rise into the air, a woman grows out of the middle of the road. First they see her short, delicate, orange hair, then her small, pale face, skinny shoulders and waist. She's wearing a long flowing nightgown that goes all the way down to her bare feet on the black pavement.

This is Braxton's mom, Mrs. Chadwick. She has something in her hand.

Dad forces Sammy off the stick. He squeezes her wrist too tight. His palm wraps over the blue and white BMW logo and grinds the gear into first. Sammy leans into the car door as Bette jerks left and then stops sideways in the middle of the road, the passenger side facing Mrs. Chadwick. She has a gun. She is wafer thin, a premonition.

Dad slams Bette into reverse and leans his arm behind Sammy's headrest. He parks in front of the Chadwick home, a small white box with blue shutters and a kid's bike leaned into a pine bush.

Dad doesn't pull the keys out of the ignition or turn Bette off.

"Stay here," he says.

A gust of warm air blows through the car when he opens the door.

Only he knows why he gets out of the car.

Mrs. Chadwick kneels on her front lawn, swaying forward and backward on her knees. Her hands are hidden, squished between her thighs. She stands as he approaches. Where her knees had pressed the floral fabric of her gown into the lawn are two oval grass stains. The early morning sun shines through the thin material, revealing her skinny, bony body.

She points the small gun at him.

He reaches both hands out and away from him. Her lips stretch taut across her gums.

The motor idles too loudly for Sammy to hear what Mrs. Chadwick is saying. She thinks about rolling down all the windows but doesn't want to hear her Dad if the bullet were to blow through his belly.

Sammy closes her eyes.

She wonders where Braxton is. She pictures him at the

bus stop, standing with his hands in his pockets and his Asteroid M. lunchbox in his yellow backpack; the bus rolling up to the corner of Bren Mar Drive and Hershey, its doors opening with a hiss as the stop sign swings out, and Braxton steps off the curb. Then, like he always does, Braxton forms his lips in a kiss on his left hand and then pats his palm on the side of the bus as he boards. Once Sammy asked why he does this, and he said, "My mom says it's good luck to kiss doors."

Sammy kisses both of her hands in the soft spot where fingers meet palm and presses them into the door window. Maybe if she presses real hard the luck might work better. She presses and presses and the gun fires but Sammy does not look. She can't look. Try as she might her eyes won't open. She does not want to see what has become of her dad.

Birds trill overhead where eyes of god blink in a blue, cloudless sky. Down below the gun slips from Mrs. Chadwick's hand and lands on the lawn. He stands behind her with arms grasping around her middle. He clings to her body like a child to a rag doll. He lowers her to the ground and sits with his legs sticking out straight in front of him. He pulls her across his lap, hugging her into his chest. She smells like a hot bath.

He rocks her from side to side, back and forth before heaving in a deep breath. Her head lolls to one side and comes to rest on his shoulder. She murmurs. He takes her face in his hands, and turns her head side to side. There is no blood and she is so precious and fragile and broken.

The guilt comes last. He looks up and sees Sammy's tiny hands and rectangle nose pushed flat against the car window, her eyes closed like two small fists.

RAZ-JAN

One glance at his father could give Baraz a stomachache. A quiet teenager, he was most comfortable when those around him were happy, which might account for why Baraz felt unwell when he pulled into the drive. Pedar, a tall man with broad but lean shoulders, paced behind the glowing, blind-drawn window on the first floor of the brick and vinyl house. He stopped in the middle of the window frame. Something about the way Pedar's spine arched made Baraz feel his father's sadness.

Baraz knew this sight well.

Pedar had spent his whole life with his big flat nose stuck in a book. He would tell Baraz to read Faulkner, and Baraz would read Faulkner. He would tell Baraz to read Woolf and Baldwin, and Baraz would read Woolf and Baldwin. He even would give Baraz the shit Chicano writers he grew up on in Los Angeles, and Baraz read them, too. "You'll find your answers here," he'd say, and his son would read it.

How do you speak to a man who loves English, who loves a language so much? It's sad to have nothing between you and your father but someone else's words. Everything from your own mouth sounds like a disappointment.

Ever Lorning. Now she was someone he could please. He liked pressing his chest against the backs of her thighs and his forehead against the wall of his Trans Am's back seat. Ever kept her hands on the small of his back and pulled him into her as if he was the only thing weighing her down. When they had finished, she swiped his dark hair out of his eyes and pulled her white T-shirt down over her small breasts, the pits completely soaked through with sweat.

"What does your name mean?" she asked. Her questions always made her seem young and naïve, though at seventeen she was only a year younger than him. He knew she found his tan skin, his delicate, almond lips, and his thick, dark brows exotic because once she had said he smelled like licorice.

He never wanted to indulge her with answers. Besides, what did he know about Iran? But the way she looked up at him, only her white T-shirt and a layer of sweat between them, biting her bottom lip as if projecting her own simple-mindedness, Baraz couldn't help himself. He wanted to tell her things he had never said to anyone.

"It means 'exalted' in Persian. It means my dad wants me to be better than what I am," he said, sitting up and tying a knot in the end of the used condom. He leaned over her, rolled down the passenger-side window, and tossed the condom onto the sidewalk.

"I'm pregnant," Ever said.

A lump swelled in his esophagus. The car suddenly felt small and dirty. Ever felt small and dirty under him. He scrambled off her and searched for his jeans.

"Baraz?" She pulled on her shorts, too.

They sat on the leather bench seat in silence. Outside, the streetlights drenched hard cement in cold light. A freight train whistled somewhere past the trees, beyond an abandoned parking lot.

How could this happen? They only had a problem once, when the condom slipped off and Ever went fishing for it. Baraz used some of the cash his father had given him for a new car muffler and paid for the morning-after pill himself.

"I'm pregnant," Ever said again.

"I heard you the first time."

"I'm sorry." Something about the way she said it, as if it was the only thing to fill the empty space between them, hardened the lump in his throat. She sounded like he did whenever he apologized to his father.

He rubbed a hand on her pale, light-haired thigh and said, "I'm sorry, too."

"I don't have any money."

Of course she couldn't keep it. Neither of them could raise a kid. Anyway, he didn't love her.

Not knowing what else to do, he kissed her. She tasted like salt and honeysuckle.

When she slipped out of the Trans Am, she said, "We'll figure it out," but the words left with her.

Baraz drove recklessly, missing the turn toward home,. His hands tightened around the steering wheel at the thought of his father's tired face.

What Hadi Elahi remembered most about his first day in America was the smell of the Pacific Ocean when he climbed out of his uncle's van. The sweet, peppery scent of sand and Mexican food made his nostrils tingle. Though his wife, Ashleigh, hated Mexican food, her potato tacos with refried beans and sugared plantains would overwhelm the house every Sunday night, without fail. It made living in Virginia a little more bearable.

He hadn't wanted to leave California but a job was a job, and teaching English literature at George Washington University was more than only that. It was opportunity. You do not pass up opportunity, at least that's what he tried to tell Baraz—what even he had trouble believing—when he explained why they had to move across the country to the suburbs of Washington, D.C.

Truth be told, Baraz was distant even before the relocation, but Hadi liked to blame his son's rebellion on a change in environment. Why wouldn't a son hate his father for moving him away from his life? Hadi thought Baraz might come around to living here, but he had resigned himself to the fact that his son hated him.

"I don't even care anymore," he said to his wife. "I really don't. He doesn't want to come to dinner? Fine."

"Maybe that's why he doesn't," Ashleigh said. "Because he thinks you don't care." She placed a tray of tacos between his stacks of papers and fat books on the kitchen table. She set a white plate for Baraz at the empty seat across from him. Hadi pictured her without her long, dirty-blonde hair, parted perfectly in the middle and framing her narrow, perpendicular features. Every part of her face pointed upwards—the slope of her nose, the top of her chin—everything but her diamond-shaped eyes.

Hadi frowned. "I never pissed off my parents this much when I was young."

"No, just when you married me."

"That was different."

"How?"

Hadi didn't know the answer to this question. Maybe it was simply rhetorical.

Ashleigh raised a skinny eyebrow. She scooped two tacos onto his plate. "He loves you, you know," she said. "He's just scared of you."

She removed a salad from the fridge and they ate their separate meals in silence. It bothered him how easily Ashleigh appeared to manage on pure instinct, and how her instincts were almost always right. He knew he had to talk to his son and set boundaries, but really, there was nothing he could do about it now. Baraz showed no signs of coming home tonight.

Baraz drove all the way to Lake Barcroft, circling it several times before finally parking his car by a wooden dock. His weekly allowance was only enough to pay for gas and a shitty pink-tray lunch at school. No extra to save for fun, much less for emergencies.

On the other side of the small lake, a young couple wearing glowing orange life jackets pushed a paddleboat into the black water. The moonlight caught in the girl's blonde hair. Baraz imagined these two lying in beds, unable to bear being home, staring at their dark ceilings before deciding to sneak out. He imagined them giggling to one another as they paddled, happy to thieve what very well might be their neighbor's boat, happy to get away for one night. Then, as the couple disappeared under a low wooden bridge in the distance:

Steal it.

Steal the money.

Ever's parents had money. He knew the screen was broken on the window by the Lornings' front door. All he needed to do was crawl around the oversized pine bush and push the windowpane in. His left arm would be long enough to reach the front door's lock. He'd seen Ever do it once when she forgot her house keys. The plan, in the end, came about simply as a matter of convenience.

Well after midnight, Baraz crouched in the trees across the street from the Lorning's perfectly white house. All the lights were off. Just one thing left to work out: What happened once he got inside?

He had no way of knowing that as he was reaching through the window, Mr. Lorning sat up in bed craving a glass of milk.

Mr. Lorning crept downstairs wearing only his underwear when, from the landing looking down the six steps into the dining room, he saw a dark, hazy shape grab something off the dining room table. The figure stopped, silhouetted by the open front door, and though his vision was blurry, Mr. Lorning could see the figure's white teeth grimace dumbly up at him.

"Stop, or I'll call the police."

With Mrs. Lorning's purse under his left arm, Baraz froze. A faint light from the doorway behind him pooled on the hardwood floor, stopping at the base of the stairs. Baraz looked up into the darkness. Though he could just barely make out Mr. Lorning's massive frame, he had recognized the deep, rolling voice instantly.

He suddenly felt stupid for stealing from people who knew him, who knew where he lived and how to find him. God, he should have at least worn a mask. There was no point in running now. Surely Mr. Lorning had recognized his daughter's boyfriend.

Mr. Lorning's big, round beer belly swayed to one side when he took a step down the stairs. He held the hint of a hand out in front of him and said, "You don't want to do this, son."

Son? The image of Ever growing a belly to match her father's came to mind. He was a son. He could not imagine having one of his own.

Baraz hugged the heavy, brown leather bag to his chest and wondered what Ever would do when she found out about this.

Mr. Lorning stepped closer. "Please, just put that down." His right hand turned from charcoal to ghostly white as it emerged from the shadow of the stairwell. "Please," Mr. Lorning said again, his voice quivering. His hand shook just a little.

He was scared, but why? Couldn't he see that Baraz didn't have anything to threaten him with? Besides, Mr. Lorning was a huge hawk of a man. He could easily beat Baraz if it came to a fight.

Mr. Lorning took the last stair and fully entered the light of the dining room. Baraz's long, skinny shadow fell onto Mr. Lorning's massive frame. Mr. Lorning had thick, stocky legs and a chest full of curled-wire hair. His underwear looked a size too small. Baraz lingered momentarily on the spot where the shadow of his skull hit Mr. Lorning's scruffy Adam's apple before reluctantly looking into his squinty snow-blue eyes.

How strange. They didn't seem to look at him, but straight through him, past the door, out to the front lawn. Baraz wondered if Mr. Lorning knew about the condom he'd thrown out there on the sidewalk earlier that night.

"We can figure this out," Mr. Lorning said, sliding one bare foot forward over the hardwood floor and twisting his outstretched arm so his palm faced upward. "Just give it to me," he said.

Baraz loosened his grip around the purse, and held it out by its long, skinny strap. The dining room walls shrunk in towards the bag's weight, as if gravity had shifted. Mr. Lorning reached out towards the purse. Baraz closed his eyes and felt his heartbeat consume his skull, waiting for his life to collapse in on itself under all this weight.

"What's your name, son?"

His name? Baraz lurched out of his terror. Mr. Lorning couldn't remember his name? Baraz looked at the purse, then back into Mr. Lorning's eyes. He pulled the purse to his chest, suddenly recognizing the strangeness in those eyes. Mr. Lorning wasn't wearing his glasses. Mr. Lorning could not see him clearly. The brave man had confronted a stranger, a thief, while virtually blind. He had no idea it was his daughter's boyfriend staring him straight in the face.

The weight in Baraz's feet lifted and he sprinted through the door behind him, still clutching the stolen property, his arms pumping faster than his legs could carry him. He slipped through the trees across the street, leaving Mr. Lorning standing on his cement stoop, yelling into the humid night. By the time Baraz reached the open expanse of the abandoned parking lot on the other side of the wood, his lungs were burning. His lips stretched into a crooked smile as he started his car. It wasn't until he pulled into his parents' driveway that he noticed his hands had been shaking.

The hard taco shells had turned soggy by the time Baraz shuffled into the kitchen, hands dug into his wrinkled jeans' pockets, a scowl deepening. He had hidden the stolen purse in his black backpack, which hung from one shoulder.

"It's late," Pedar said. He stood at the kitchen counter, pushing a bag of tea into his mug with the back of a spoon. He looked old sipping tea like that, with cream that turned the drink gray like his short, dead hair.

"Zan is already sleeping," he said.

Baraz hated how his father called Mom wife in Persian. *Zan is asleep. Zan cooks what I like. Zan always listens.* It sounded old-fashioned coming from a man who married a white woman.

"Mom hates tacos," Baraz said, spotting the cold tray of food on the kitchen table. He wiped the sweat from his forehead with the nook of his elbow, then slid his hand back into his pocket.

"Still, she made them," Pedar said, but all Baraz heard was: *Zan does what I ask her to do. Why don't you?*

"It's three a.m." His father pulled out his chair at the kitchen table and sat, nodding at the empty plate across from him.

Baraz slid his backpack off his shoulder and made sure to place it between his feet when he sat down. Pedar felt so far away, behind his books and papers set neatly out in front of him, the stack of papers on the left covered in red pen, the stack on the right, clean. Pedar's reading glasses lay over the essay he had been in the middle of grading.

"You didn't mow the lawn." Meaning: *Where were you?*

"I forgot," Baraz said.

"You forgot your father?" *What was so important that you'd forget your pedar?* He rubbed his temples. The lines of his crow's-feet stretched out, then reformed a little further from the corner of his eyes.

This simple gesture struck a nerve in Baraz—his father's sadness made the piled papers look less white, the books more worn and tattered, even the leftover tacos were sad—and it was all he could do to say, "I'm sorry," and, "I'll do it tomorrow." Feeling the brick of his backpack at his feet, Baraz half-wanted to ask about being paid to mow the lawn.

"There are leftovers," Pedar said.

"I'm not hungry." Baraz pushed back his chair, the legs making a quick, chirping whine as they dragged across the linoleum floor. Baraz leaned over to pick up his backpack from under the chair.

"Raz-jan?"

Baraz rose to his father whispering the distant but familiar nickname. He hadn't heard it in so long.

Raz.

He hadn't heard that name since he was a little kid running across the hot sand in California. When or why his father stopped calling him that, he couldn't remember—*Raz*. He thought of Ever and wondered what nickname he would give his son, if it was a son. That is, if they were to keep it, which they weren't. Hearing this nickname for the first time in so long, Baraz almost dared himself to speak these secrets, to tell Pedar everything.

"Raz, do you hate me?" his father asked.

"I do not hate you," Baraz said.

What he wanted to say: *I don't know how to tell you anything about my life.*

Pedar turned from him, dumping his tea into the kitchen sink. The steam rose up, and Baraz climbed the stairs to his bedroom.

Hadi went back to his papers, but after getting halfway through one essay, his mind traveled west to California.

They used to sit on the edge of the boardwalk wearing matching sneaker sandals—Raz's feet a smaller version of his own—that swung back and forth over the sand as they played their game.

Hadi told long stories that his son ate up. When he stopped mid-sentence, usually on a noun, Raz would smush Hadi's face delicately with little fingertips, contorting his lips into strange, unfamiliar shapes. A sound would creak deep in Hadi's throat, calling up a word that would change the course of whatever tale he was spinning.

Raz would laugh. Then: "More, Father. More, please!"

How he wished his son would still say, "More, Father, more, please," whenever he handed him a new book to read. But Baraz didn't, not anymore.

This, he thought, as his head slowly drooped forward, he would never have again. His left cheek pressed flat against the stack of graded papers on the kitchen table. His mind opened to the California shore slammed with waves, and Raz giggling, "More, Father. Please. More!"

A gust of wind runs through his thick, black hair, but the child doesn't notice it. The water moves up to Hadi's feet. One of Raz's sandals slips off, splashes in the water and floats away, a receding fleck of orange until the undertow sucks it down and it disappears into the next onslaught.

The water collects, heavier, colder, and faster than before. Soon the waves are up to Hadi's chest and Raz's neck. Still, his son mouths the words: *More, Father. More!* And Baraz is completely submerged.

Panicked, Hadi inhales a gulp of air and dives under for his boy. The water stings his nostrils. He shuts his eyes against the cold, but forces them open when he feels his son's tiny fingers pinch his cheeks.

Everything is calm.

The entire beach is underwater. It's as if he is looking out through a pair of blue-tinted glasses. No one else has noticed the phenomenon, least of all Raz, who mouths, "More, Father. More stories," and claps twice, four air bubbles floating from his lips up towards the sky.

Hadi wants his son to notice what is happening to the world.

"Look! Look!" he screams, but his voice comes out as sludge.

"More!" Raz pokes his index finger to Hadi's lips and smiles a toothless grin.

"No. Look what has happened." He grabs Raz by the wrists and shakes him. He feels his eyes cry and wonders if tears are different than oceans.

"Look! We're underwater! We aren't even breathing," he screams.

He squeezes both of his son's shoulders and shakes him even more violently. Raz's face is a blank stare of bewilderment—his features, just like his mother's, pointing up toward the watery sky.

Hadi Elahi woke in a puddle of drool collecting on his papers. He washed his hands and flicked off the kitchen light before going to bed.

Upstairs, he stopped at his son's bedroom. Light leaked out from under the door. He hoped Baraz was reading. He knocked and heard no response. He waited a moment before entering.

A lamp sitting on a wooden desk pushed up against the window of the far wall gave everything in the small room a warm, yellow tinge. Posters of old cars hung from the wall opposite a twin bed. Baraz sat at the foot of the bed, a brown leather purse in his lap, his eyes wide and guilty.

Baraz turned to hide the purse behind him, but he was caught.

My son, a thief? No, Hadi thought. He would not steal from his mother. There had to be some explanation.

"Knock, why don't you?" his son said.

"If you have something to hide, why didn't you lock the door?"

"I shouldn't have to." Baraz sucked his bottom lip, exposing his wide, white teeth.

"Don't be a smart-ass."

"I'm sorry," said his son.

"Are you sorry for being a smart-ass, or for stealing your mother's purse?"

Baraz pushed the bag farther behind him on the bed.

"Don't be stupid," Hadi said.

Baraz's oval face grew blank. He looked so much like his mother. Hadi saw nothing of himself there.

"Sorry," Zan's son said.

"Sorry you got caught?"

"Sorry for everything."

Hadi sat next to Baraz. He didn't know how to reach out to him. Hadi had tried to share his work with Baraz, but evidently that wasn't enough.

"Do you need money?"

Baraz looked down at his knees and shook his head.

"Is it money?" Hadi asked again.

This time Baraz nodded.

"Are you in trouble?"

"No."

"Why do you feel you need to steal, then?"

Baraz hesitated. "It's for the car."

"How much do you need?"

Baraz shrugged.

"One hundred dollars?"

He shrugged again.

"How much?"

"A hundred. Yeah."

Hadi stood up, removed his wallet from his back pocket, and pulled out five twenties. He knew this wasn't the right thing to do. He knew he should take his son's car away. He knew he should ground him, at the very least, but he couldn't stand Baraz hating him any more than he already did. This way, he could help him.

Baraz reached for the cash and Hadi pulled his hand away.

"You can't do this," Hadi said.

"I know."

"If I give you this money, you have to apologize to your mother."

"I know."

"You have to see that disappointed look on her face when you give her back her purse—"

"Okay."

He handed Baraz the five crisp bills.

Baraz looked up at him with a sad, sullen expression and Hadi knew, or thought he knew, that Baraz really was sorry.

"Don't wake your mother. You can talk to her in the morning," Hadi said, before closing the bedroom door behind him.

*

Baraz had felt the tension in his neck and jaw, even on the roof of his mouth, the center of him aching, wanting some sort of relief. When his father closed the door, Baraz couldn't hold onto it any longer. Hot tears streamed down his face, and he sobbed. Pedar had called him stupid, and that was exactly how he felt. Stupid.

He wiped the snot from his nose, then counted the cash in Mrs. Lorning's purse again. Sixty-eight dollars. Not much. Not even close to being enough, but it was better than nothing.

In the morning, Baraz stuffed the money into an envelope, folded it in half and slid it into his back pocket. He left before his parents woke. He could talk to his mom later. His plan: ditch the purse, give Ever the money, then wash his hands of the whole ordeal. But when Ever slid into the passenger seat, Baraz reaching for her hand and knowing by the way she yanked her own hand away that it was all over between them, this plan suddenly didn't seem so good. No, this plan was lousy. Now all he wanted, more than anything, was to keep her there, in his car, for just a while longer, even if it meant lying.

"What do you have to say for yourself?"

Ever crossed her arms. Today her hair was down and swept over one shoulder. Baraz wanted to be that shoulder, to feel her ends.

Baraz's new plan: feign ignorance.

"I'm sorry," he said.

"What?"

"I'm sorry. I didn't know what to say last night."

"I thought maybe you—" she paused. Her eyes scanned his, and Baraz tried to look confused, stupid even.

"I what?" he asked, feeling the hard wad of cash in his back pocket.

"Forget it."

"Ever, I'll do whatever you want. What do you want?"

"I don't know," Ever bounced her knees up and down. She always did this to keep her thighs from sticking to his leather car seat. He felt so grateful for the familiar gesture. Baraz reached for her hand, and this time she took it.

They drove to school in silence. Finally, at a red light, Ever said, "You'll never guess what happened last night."

"What happened?" Baraz asked, leaning over to kiss her warmly on the cheek.

SOPHIE SALMON

Sophie Salmon is afraid of stethoscopes. The sight of any medical equipment whatsoever sends Sophie into a panic attack. Even a sneaking suspicion that she is sick is not enough to send her to the doctor. So Sophie makes excuses for herself. She attributes the bruises along her arms to clumsiness, her nausea to dehydration, and her general feeling of lousiness to lack of sleep. What she cannot explain away are the sudden appearance of floaters in her left eye. On bright sunny days the small dark spots pan across her field of vision and cause her eyes to water, and still she will not make an appointment with an optometrist. She did not want to know. And besides, the whole sick thing can have certain benefits, like those ten pounds she lost due to lack of appetite.

Sophie Salmon is twenty-three years old and five feet, eight inches tall, weighing one-hundred and ten pounds. She does not mind that her neck looks longer, that her cheeks are less plump and her nose appears more pointed. She particularly doesn't mind that her thighs no longer touch when she stands right foot flush against the left, or that she has to clasp the eye hooks of her bras one notch tighter. No, she does not mind at all because Sophie looks good. Sophie is a catch. Dudes want to get with her small tight little ass, or at least that is what some guy, a boy really, no older than seventeen, yells from his beat-up Chevy as she crosses Division on her way to work this morning.

No, it is not her sudden change in appearance or even that she feels lousy that frightens Sophie Salmon. What frightens her is what if she needs glasses, or has an astigmatism or diabetes or her retina is detaching from the rest of her eyeball. What if she has a tumor. What if that tumor turns out to be cancerous. What if these ailments cannot be cured. No, it is not death, exactly, but living with these things, surviving them—a changed person—that is what scares Sophie Salmon.

So when the Chevy rounds the turn onto Division, wheels crunching winter salt just feet in front of her, and the boy smiles a filthy chipped-toothed grin, Sophie Salmon cannot help but smile back at him. At least she still looks good, even in her parka. And she keeps smiling as she descends the stairs to the CTA tunnel, as she stands crammed and sweaty in an afternoon rush hour train headed for the Loop. The blue line is under construction and what used to be a simple ten minute ride to Clark and Lake now takes fifteen, a fact that Sophie usually laments—the tracks were fine! But today, that dimple of hers on her right cheek stays there all the way to work, where she finds a cheesecake on a long folding table in the center of the break room. *Good luck Jamey!* is written across the top in a swirl of blue frosting. It is not until she reads the perfect cursive that her smile disappears.

JAMEY

Jamey is insecure about his looks. He is miraculously tall. He has an unusually large lower lip, and thinks his gum to teeth ratio is off. Too much teeth, not enough gums. He has a mole on the left side of his neck and long John-Lennon-circa-Yoko-Ono hair. What he wants more than anything is to play music, but he thinks he is lousy at it. He plays some guitar and practices his scales on the shitty organ in the living room of the small coach house on Whipple that he shares with four roommates. His most prized possession is his record player. His least prized possession is the fine art degree in graphic design he got from some school no one cares about. Why? Because for the two years since school he has worked at the stupid Borders on Mag Mile selling people books they will most likely never read.

Thank god he is getting out. Thank god this is his last day ever. Thank god, thank god, thank god, he thinks every time the cash register slams shut. Then he sees Sophie rushing in behind the counter ten minutes late. His chest feels like a sack of sand when he thinks that today might be the last day he ever sees her in those ratty converse shoes with star laces.

Two weeks ago, Jamey noticed purple bags under Sophie's eyes, the way her shoulders hunched over the drawer of cash when she made change, how her skin stretched taut over bones. Today when he looks at her from three registers away he thinks he can hear her stomach grumble. He'd like to take her out for a large, very large hamburger but he recalls reading somewhere that people with eating disorders are touchy about being invited to dinner. Maybe she just needs a hug. For a moment he actually considers walking up to her and hugging her, but before he can, a woman in a white blouse and pencil skirt steps up to the counter. When he hands her her change, the tips of their fingers accidentally touch, and the moment is gone. Who is he kidding anyway? He will never talk to Sophie Salmon ever again.

During his break, Jamey goes outside to smoke a cigarette in front of the Water Tower. It looks like a sacred object, an old castle in the middle of a glass city. The weather is freezing, but he smokes two more while listening to a street performer with long dreadlocks pick at an acoustic guitar.

A small girl bundled up in an oversized puffy coat stands nearby, the silver ribbon of a blue balloon clutched tightly in her mitten hand. She walks up to the man when he finishes a song, gives him the balloon, and then quickly scurries back to her adoring parents.

Jamey thinks: Wow. And: That's so brave. And: Fuck it, I need to say something to Sophie.

When he gets back from his break, Sophie is ringing out a copy of *Twilight* to a grey-haired man with a high widow's peak and skinny cleft chin. Jamey stands behind her and waits for the end of the transaction. The florescent lights make her pale skin look almost translucent. He wonders why a man with a cleft chin wants to read *Twilight*. Sophie gives the man incorrect change—one dime, four nickels and two pennies instead of one dime, two nickels and four pennies—but Jamey does not correct the error.

When she has finished, he taps her on the shoulder.

Jamey asks: "Want to do something later?"

Sophie says: "Okay."

They both think: It's about time.

A BRIEF HISTORY LESSON

Three months ago, when Sophie said goodbye to Jamey at the train station he kissed her. She liked the way he didn't try to slip his tongue down her throat. The next night, Sophie invited him back to her apartment. They got naked but did not have sex. A week later, when they did have sex, Jamey made weird, soft grunting noises. They did not freak Sophie out. She actually found them both adorable and very flattering.

Jamey liked the way Sophie bit his ear, not at the lobe, but higher and further in around the cartilage.

In the morning, Sophie could not stop herself from thinking that the only reason Jamey fucked her was because he got too drunk. Jamey feared the only reason a beautiful girl like Sophie would sleep with him was because she got too drunk. At work they both pretended that nothing happened.

That same day Jamey thought he heard Sophie talking to August, their manager, about the size of his penis. Sophie actually made a comment about a set of sparkly mini pencils on display next to the cash registers. She found them tacky and Jamey lost a lot of sleep.

They have not hung out since.

When Jamey landed a graphic design job with a small Chicago press, he stopped thinking about Sophie before going to sleep at night. Exhausted from working two jobs for the past month, he would collapse stomach-down on his mattress on the floor, no box spring. No bed frame. As he fell asleep, his only thought would be: Fuck! I've got to do this all again tomorrow.

Today, when Jamey finally asks Sophie out again on his very last day of work, Sophie thinks: About time. She also thinks: Just a booty call. But that would be okay. Lately she has been lonely, she hasn't had sex in a while, she feels like a shitty carp and not a pink salmon, and maybe, maybe Jamey can help her out. Also she thinks: Dude looks good in plaid.

FINALLY. . .

At a quarter past 9 p.m., Sophie steals L fare from her till before counting the drawer. In the break room she eyes the remaining crumbs of cheese cake on the long folding table. She is not hungry, despite having eaten only half a peanut butter and jelly sandwich and an apple today, washing them down with three cups of coffee. She slides her backpack over her right shoulder. Tomorrow morning, she will wipe the fog off her bathroom mirror and see a big purple bruise on the same shoulder. It will be a sign that she is getting sicker, a sign she will have a hard time ignoring as she blow dries her hair and smudges eye liner on her bottom lids.

Outside, the wind stings like a paper cut. Jamey stands against the building, a cigarette resting on his lower lip and hands dug into blue jeans. Sophie flashes the universal sign for smoking with the thumb and paw of her purple mitten, and that's how she smokes the cigarette on the silent walk to the train.

Six blocks later, they turn right onto Kinzie and crane their heads like tourists up at the Trump Tower construction. Sophie holds her right hand up to the sky and covers the building with the butt of her cigarette. She closes one eye, and the building plays peek-a-boo.

"Isn't it beautiful?" Jamey asks.

"Yeah. If you like steel and concrete," Sophie says dropping her cigarette on the ground and stepping on it.

"You don't think it's beautiful?"

Sophie thinks the tower looks like a giant metallic lighter, or a lipstick case, or a shard of glass. She thinks people want to think it is beautiful. That people want it to be art, but really it is just a building surrounded by other buildings in a city that doesn't need any more fucking buildings. It is the spinal tap of Chicago. She doesn't say any of this to Jamey.

Sophie Salmon says, "It's just a building."

"That's sad," Jamey says, and lights another cigarette with chapped red hands.

They turn left onto State and cross the river. The tower guts the horizon behind them now, and waits to be crowned with a lightning rod.

ON THE TRAIN

Sophie leans her head against the window and feels it vibrate against her temple. She feels better now than she has in weeks and doesn't want the ride to end. She thinks she knows what will happen. The way Jamey tucks his long hair behind his ears will kill her. The way his vowels go long and open when he gets drunk will kill her. The way he walks, or blinks or leans against buildings when he smokes will kill her and she won't be able to help it. She'll let him fuck her and he won't talk to her for a month, maybe longer. Maybe never again. After all, they are no longer co-workers as of twenty minutes ago.

Sophie closes her eyes, and the moment she does, Jamey realizes the one thing he likes about her most, more than anything, more than the way she bites his ear, more than her ruler straight black hair or her cute little shoes, is how comfortable he feels sitting next to her in silence. Not needing to say anything. Just looking at her slender face and neck as they rock with the movements of the train car. He fights the urge to reach over and grab her tiny mittened hand.

AT A BAR ON WESTERN AVENUE

It smells like Clorox and sweat. The coat hooks lining the wall opposite the bar are overloaded with jackets and scarves. A single spotlight illuminates a man sporting two braided pigtails and a white bass. No one in the cramped bar is listening to him play. In the hour Sophie and Jamey are cramped toward the back of the bar, Sophie drinks one Pabst and two glasses of water, and eats half of the soggy leftover peanut butter and jelly sandwich from her backpack. Jamey drinks three Pabst and two shots of Beam.

They talk about nothing either of them really cares about, mainly the store and how their supervisor kind of sucks a ton of dicks.

"I fucking hate it when she sprays that raspberry shit all over the break room," Jamey yells over the music.

"Yeah." Sophie sips her water. "She kind of sucks a ton of dicks," she says.

"Like, actually?"

"No. I just mean she sucks."

"Oh yeah. Right." Jamey tucks a long strand of hair behind his ear and Sophie prepares to die.

"I'm so glad I'm out of there."

"Yeah," Sophie says, her lip curling downward.

Jamey orders a fourth beer, and points at Sophie. "Want one?"

"No, it's too crowded in here." She leans against the bar.

Claudio, the neighborhood tamale guy, holds his red cooler above the crowd and shouts, "Hot tamales!"

Jamey pulls a five out of his velcro wallet.

"No," Sophie says. "Let's get out of here."

"You sure?"

The lock of hair slips from behind Jamey's ear.

"Yes, I'm sure."

They leave the fourth beer untouched on the bar top.

AROUND THE CORNER

Sophie Salmon lives on Thomas, in the first floor rear unit of a three-floor flat. She makes Jamey stay in the living room, where the sole window faces the rear entrance of a Subway. The walls of the room are bare and the furniture is second-hand. Jamey sits on the sofa and crosses and uncrosses his legs.

From her room down the hall Sophie hears the familiar squeak of the couch. She slips off her jeans and searches for a clean pair of pajama pants in the piles of laundry scattered across the hardwood floor. She smells three pairs before resigning herself to semi-clean ones with a horrible leopard pattern. She slides them on over her boney hips and shoves the laundry under her bed. In her open closet hang fifty or sixty unused plastic hangers.

Sophie feels like her body is wilting. For this reason she lets Jamey press her body between his and the mattress in the dark like an old buttercup between the pages of a heavy book. They lay and kiss like this for a while, Sophie reaching her arms around him, feeling his shoulder blades through his shirt. When he arches his back to unbutton his shirt, his pelvis digs into her. She holds on hard but he's strong and now his shirt is off. Jamey buries his face into her neck. She licks his ear and he breathes heavily, his whole body tensing until she stops. Then Jamey slips a hand down between the elastic of her pajama bottoms and her white cotton underwear.

Sophie thinks: This is all he wants me for.

She grabs his wrist, forces his hand away and lies. "I don't have a condom."

"That's okay." Jamey pushes himself up onto his arms, his hands pressing into the mattress as he looks down at her. "There are other things we can do."

"No," she says.

Jamey rolls off of her and lies on his back, resting his wrists crisscross on his forehead. They stare at the ceiling in silence for a long time.

Finally Jamey asks, "Do you want me to go home?"

"Do you want to go home?" Sophie asks.

"No. But that's not what I asked. Do you want me to go?"

"No."

"Okay."

"It's just that I'm—" she pauses. "Never mind."

"What?"

"It's been a month since you even talked to me."

"I'm sorry," Jamey says. "I have a tendency to forget that other people exist when I'm busy," he lies.

Sophie wants to say: *If you liked me enough, if you really liked me, it wouldn't matter how busy you are.* Instead she says, "I think I'm the one that's always running out of time."

"What do you mean?"

"I think I'm really sick."

Jamey rolls onto his left shoulder so he can face her and props himself up on an elbow.

"Have you gone to the doctor?"

"No."

"Then how do you know?"

"I just do."

In this moment Jamey realizes that yes, he really fucking likes Sophie Salmon and he doesn't want anything bad to happen to her. Instead of doing the easy thing, he holds her small crooked body in his arms. Soon the black sky outside the window lightens and he notices Sophie is struggling to stay awake.

"Sophie. I'm going to lie on my right side so I don't snore. It's not that I don't want to face you, okay? I just thought I should let you know."

"Okay."

IN THE MORNING

Sophie and Jamey share a glass of orange juice. Sophie is too tired to walk so they take the bus to the L stop. They climb to the landing where the stairs split, one set heading to O'Hare, the other to Forest Park. Jamey puts a hand on her shoulder.

"Sophie, you know I'll go with you."

"Where?"

"To the doctor."

"You will?"

"Yes."

The track begins to rattle above them. Jamey leans forward and kisses Sophie Salmon on the temple. They turn and climb the rest of the stairs alone.

FELECIA SASSAFRAS IS FICTION

A secret: Felecia Sassafras is disappearing. The truth: If Felecia Sassafras were to ask, that is, if she were to break her number one rule—don't tell anyone this secret—if she were to ask a doctor, a therapist, a philosopher, they would all say the same thing. They would say, "You are becoming invisible." Felecia, however, does not understand the subtle difference between seeing nothing and nothingness itself because I am telling you, Felecia Sassafras is fiction.

How it works: She cannot see a small sliver of her right calf, both of her bald knee caps and the tips of each of her delicate index fingers, but that does not mean they are not there.

Felecia can still tie her shoes and press doorbells, only now the adjectives soft, hard, rough, slick, dry, wet, hot, cold and hundreds of others are all but lost to her transparent appendages.

She picks up a rock and instead of feeling its shape, its arches and ridges, she feels its age. She lifts her fingers towards the sun and can tell that the solar system is not happy today. She suspects it almost never is.

At home: Felecia Sassafras touches the television screen during the evening news and when particularly devastating things stream across the screen—a natural disaster, another suicide bombing, a house fire—her fingers are such sorrowful things. This is why she wears gloves even though it is summer. I tell her not to worry, that I have it all under control, but she just cries and cries and cries.

What has yet to disappear: Felecia Sassafrass' wide hips, narrow shoulders, and the prominent zig-zag wrinkle that travels from the bridge of her nose to the curve of her widow's peak.

Lately: I have been ignoring Felecia Sassafras because she won't stop crying. She won't stop crying because she is fiction. She complains that she is not real and asks stupid questions, like "Why am I disappearing?" When I tell her that it is none of her concern, she does some cliché gesture. She crosses her arms or falls to the floor, her eyes turning into two watering stop signs.

Instead of hanging with Felicia Sassafras: I have been watching a lot of porn, mainly girl on girl action because the feminist in me hates to a see a daughter get rammed. I like the retro stuff because of the bushes. It just seems way more real, unlike Felicia. She looks like a little girl down there.

Today: When I fire up the laptop, Felicia Sassafras is hanging out in the upper lefthand corner of the screen. Her mouth looks like a manila folder. She whispers, "My left foot is gone."

"It is not gone," I say. "You just can't see it."

"I lost it last night while you were busy watching those gross, ugly sluts."

"They aren't gross."

"Why are you so lazy?" she asks.

Even though I have promised myself I will spend all day with Felicia Sassafras, I point at her and say, "Shut up," before slamming the laptop closed. Then I turn on the television and swear I will only watch one episode and only smoke the tiniest bit of grass.

A month-old potato: Is not the best smoking device, but I'm not complaining. Sure, it smells of rot and sweat, and it will probably sprout a plant any day now, but so what?

I know: Felecia Sassafras is disappearing, or becoming invisible, or whatever the fuck is going on. I know that after I watch *The Wire* I will come back to find her in Baltimore, and after I watch *Mad Men* she will suddenly have a shitty husband. I will tell her to stop being so stupid and sad, and she will say, "It is your fault. I am stupid because you are stupid.

I am sad because you are sad." I know she is right, and still I watch another episode.

Don't you think: Felecia Sassafras is just too much work? That I should at least start entertaining the idea of wiping her out altogether?

By the time the fat Papa John's delivery guy knocks on my apartment door: I have watched one hour of porn, two episodes of *Mad Men*, one episode of *The Wire*, and I am feeling pretty guilty. So fine. So Felecia wins.

Felecia Sassafras needs to: get a divorce, move back to the District, find a friend, and grow a bush. I promise her happiness and good looks if she just listens to me. She gladly divorces the asshole—some guy I have never met, which seems weird—but she fights me on everything else. She boards a train in Baltimore but it breaks down before it pulls into D.C. I tell her to hail a yellow cab and take it the remaining twenty miles. Instead, like the little brat she is, Felecia Sassafras throws down fifty-eight bucks on a room at a Motel 8. The room smells like sour cigars. The first thing she does is pull off her too-tight blue jeans and white tanktop. Now she is naked, save for her two black gloves.

In the yellow-streaked shower: Felecia Sassafras shaves off the small blond stubble on her pelvis. As she stands there rocking from her visible right foot to her invisible left foot, the lukewarm water hitting the curve of her back, I tell her to at least go to a bar, maybe meet someone nice, but no. She is too embarrassed.

She says, "I hate you." She says, "I can't believe you told the whole world my secret."

"Not the whole world," I say. "Just them."

"Yeah," Felecia says, "And now they all know I am disappearing."

"You are not disappearing," I say. "You are becoming invisible."

"What's the difference?" Felecia cries, falling to the floor of the bathtub like a mascara-streaked drama queen. The pink razor slips out of her gloved hand and slides to the moldy shower drain. For a second I think she might snatch the Bic and slit her wrists.

"I am not suicidal. I don't even know if I would bleed," she sniffles. "And by the way, can't you think of a better word than 'moldy'? Moldy is so boring. Moldy is so cliché."

I tell her to shut up and the second I do, her whole left arm is gone. All that remains is the dark red socket of her rotator cuff.

Like any normal person: I give up.

Of course: I should probably invest in a real pipe, or some rolling papers at the very least. My potato is starting to sprout stems, so I use the only remaining index page from my only copy of *Leaves of Grass*. I smoke it while watching a small asian chick rub one out.

My favorite porno: *Sluts on Sluts on Sluts*. I do not mastur-
bate when I watch *Sluts on Sluts on Sluts*. I am not into mas-
turbating. I just like staring like a total creep. Like a lurker,
always there but never participating. And unlike Felicia Sassafras, the sluts in *Sluts on Sluts on Sluts* do not shave their
pubic hair, do not cry and do not know that I myself am
watching. At least, I hope they do not know.

Later: "They know you are watching," Felicia Sassafras
says. She has finally pulled herself out of the shower and
is sitting cross legged on the browning, hotel bedspread
with a towel wrapped around her middle. She bounces her
invisible foot up and down and tongues a stick of red bubble gum.

"How do you know?" I ask.

"I just do."

"You just do? No, that's not how this works."

"Whatever you say."

Felicia Sassafras has a nasty grin.

There, between her two thin lips, is nothing but red
tongue and gums, and gum. Her teeth have vanished. I must
make an awful face because Felicia Sassafras' brown eyes grow
wide and she covers her mouth with a gloved hand. She runs
to the bathroom where she cries and cries and cries while
looking at her reflection in the toothpaste-speckled mirror.

"You just had to put toothpaste on the mirror, didn't
you?" Felecia asks.

"What do you mean?"

"You just had to rub it in?"

"I'm not sorry," I say.

I'm not sorry because: Felecia Sassafras is fiction, Felecia Sassafras is stupid, Felecia Sassafras is the least observant character ever.

Look: Felecia Sassafras is chewing like a cow as she cleans the toothpaste off the mirror with bits of toilet paper. See how her jaw pops out slightly as she chomps down. Hear the smack of the Wrigley, the pop of a bubble. Felecia Sassafras doesn't even realize, she doesn't even notice that she can feel the slick backs of her teeth against her tongue. She thinks only that if she cannot see them, then they simply must not be there. She is just that clueless.

The last thing Felecia Sassafras says before I call it a night: Show don't tell, stupid.

The day after that, and the day after that, and the day after that: I ignore Felecia Sassafras and she loses sight of the other foot, an elbow, the mole on her left nipple, both ears, her thick ass and three inches of her long, red hair. She is so low, so forlorn, she does not feel anything the moment these parts of her fade. Sometimes it takes minutes, hours even, for her to notice that something has fled. For example, she doesn't even know about her eyebrows.

Now: All Felecia Sassafras will do is lie on the browning motel bed, a pile of her visible and invisible body parts. She looks like a deconstructed mannequin. I ask her if she wants to do something fun. Maybe get really drunk and have a one night stand. That could be interesting. But she just rolls her eyes, and the second she does her lids disappear.

Felecia moans, "Now I can't even shut out this awful place."

"Hey, this motel was your idea," I say.

Another secret: I am starting to miss the old Felecia Sassafras. I try to watch *Sluts on Sluts on Sluts*, but now all the girls just look fake, even with their extravagant pubic hair. I try to watch *Mad Men* and *The Wire*, but all I can so is daydream about her round face lying there on that bed, staring at the ceiling. God, she is so boring.

Drugs: I am starting to think they might be the only way to cure the monotony, the only way to appease Felecia Sassafras. These motel bills are adding up.

Finally I ask: "How about you develop a drug habit?"

"Oh, like you?"

"Weed isn't habit-forming," I say.

"You would say that, wouldn't you?"

"What's that supposed to mean?"

"That you're predictable."

I cross my arms. "Well, then what do you want to do?"

"Nothing," Felecia Sassafras says. "I want to do nothing."

"Nothing?"

"Yes, nothing."

And with that, all that's left is a floundering head and half of a right boob.

Poor girl: She wastes away like this all day.

Now the motel is lonely: Two black gloves lay neatly on the bed. Felecia Sassafras is gone and I don't feel anything for the departed.

Then: A horrible thing happens. My lazy left thumb flees, leaving white bone and red and red, and red.

NIGHT HAWK

That night, a terrible thing rose up out of our silence and chose me.

AJ must have also felt it lingering in the salty smell of his old Jeep. I feared he could see how I saw him: a hard curve for a chin, too much purple under the eyes and—his most distinguishing feature—a sliver of hot air between his two front teeth. He sucked down a No. 27 and pushed smoke through his gap as we turned onto Little River Turnpike, the glowing IHOP sign towering over miles of drenched strip malls in the distance. Had I known what lay in store, I would never have begged.

I remember a few snippets of detail. The pig mouthing stop, his breath hitting the cold air and turning into fog, his outstretched hand, my foot slipping on the brake and bending sideways. The gun. The gun. The pancakes sitting heavy in my queasy stomach. Five or six loud pops. The hard vibrations of the steering wheel as I swerve left, then right over the slick parking lot. A bullet scorched my ear, somewhere behind me now. AJ's piercing scream. Nowhere left to go. The air bag punches me in the face. The last thing I remember is passing out to the smell of burning rubber and steel.

The night started like most: We had smoked all our weed and I wanted more.

"Another time," AJ said.

"I'll pay," I said.

Neither of us were in any good state to drive, but sometimes a man wants what he wants and the world owes it to him.

When we pulled into the IHOP parking lot, I pressed my cheek to the cold window. AJ clicked off the wipers and turned the rearview mirror towards the lot's only entrance. Headlights swished by and disappeared over the wet turnpike.

"Sometimes I wonder where they're all going," he said.

I said nothing.

AJ was always trying half-heartedly to move out of his parents' two-bedroom. The usual plan involved packing the bare necessities and hitching a ride to Philly with a few hundred bucks in his pocket and a list of friends' couches. He had been saying as much since he was nineteen, but here we were in our thirties still doing the same old shit we did as boys. The truth is we knew we would both die in Virginia like our fathers, and our fathers' fathers, and our fathers' fathers' fathers before them. Still, when he spoke like this, about the need within him to get out of here, a deep vessel in my gut would contract and I would wonder why he never considered that I might like to go with him.

I never knew what to say in those moments, so I clicked on the radio to DC 101.1 to kill the silence. "In the Mouth of the Dessert" by Pavement came over the speakers. Finally our dealer's high beams hit AJ across the eyes when she pulled into the lot.

My jeans were soaked through by the time we reached Abebe's boat of a car, which always smelled of skunk. A raggedy cardboard box in the back passenger-side seat forced us to sit cramped together on the sticky velour, our damp thighs pressing. I inched as far away as possible and the windows began to fog.

Abebe raised a chapped hand to her lips and the end of her cigarette lit up the side of her dark face as she inhaled. "Just a minute," she said, rolling stringy tobacco into a paper sleeve. When she was done she pressed the new cigarette to the butt of the old.

Chainsmoking rollies wasn't something you expected

from a dainty girl like Abebe. She looked breakable, but her skin flaked bark and she could snarl an easy scare. She always had her shit on lock and never double booked a deal, so we were both surprised when some girl with a hard crease between her eyebrows slid into the passenger seat and said, "Mind if we make this quick?"

Abebe made a popping sound with her tongue and her eyes rolled in the rearview. She drew a bag of weed from the center console. More than an eighth but less than a quarter. "Sixty dollars," she said to the girl.

"You said forty on the phone."

"I say sixty."

"I only have forty."

"Too bad," Abebe pulled the bag away.

The girl deflated.

AJ's elbow knocked into mine when he shoved his hand into his jean pocket and, leaning over me, waved a wet twenty in the girl's face. "You'll get me back," he said to the girl.

She snatched the twenty, and was out in the rain running to her car before saying so much as a thank you.

"Selfish girl. Always taking." Abebe began to roll another smoke.

"Who the fuck was that?" I asked.

"Don't know," AJ said.

"You just gave twenty bucks to some random chick?"

"It's just twenty bucks." AJ shrugged. That's it. Later,

when I try to brush off my dad after he pays my bail, I use the same shrug. A little shoulder raise.

I tried to ignore the wetness of my socks in my undersized shoes while AJ licked the sticky edge of a rolling paper. The turnpike lurked behind us in silence now, the sky lightening to a deep purple at the horizon. The weed hit quick and turned the world to static.

AJ took a long drag, cocked his head back, and exhaled, the smoke pouring to the ceiling. "Want to eat with us?" he said, trying to pass the smoke to Abebe. She waved it off.

"What's in it for me?"

"We'll pay," he said.

"Alright," she said.

AJ fired a shit-eating grin at me, and pinched the spliff into my hand. I couldn't help but show my disappointment. I didn't want to share my time with him. I took a drag to calm my nerves, but my pulse moved into my ears and my brain dropped into the pit of my stomach. My organs began to rise up my neck. I couldn't hold onto it any longer—I vomited into the cardboard box next to me.

"You vom in my car, you get new dealer."

AJ cackled.

All I could manage to squeak out was "I'm so sorry" before another wave rose up my throat.

Inside IHOP, the scent of pancakes caused my throat to

constrict. A black security guard by the front door nodded when we entered, every single on of his features shaped like a sharp triangle.

"Keep your head down," AJ whispered as he led me past him and into the bathroom, but I couldn't. My eyes burned. He had a gun. Must have been a cop moonlighting for the extra cash. The pig rested an uneasy hand on his gun holster.

When I finished puking orange clown fish into the toilet bowl, AJ handed me a damp paper towel and helped me to the sink. As I cupped water in my mouth to flush down the grainy, bitter taste of puke, AJ put a hand to my back.

"Don't," I said twisting away from his touch. I immediately regretted it when I saw disgust wrinkle into the narrow eyes of his mirror's reflection.

I leaned over to swallow another gulp of water. I couldn't bear to look at my own reflection and see what kind of state I was in. By the feel of it my whole face had caved in.

"Go away," I said down into the sink bowl.

AJ pushed open the bathroom door, letting in the sounds of ice cubes falling into plastic cups and waiters yelling out orders. "I can't stand that look in your eye, man," he said. "It creeps me out."

Then he was gone.

I took another gulp of tap.

*

Abebe and AJ sat next to each other at a booth by the front windows. Dawn light threatened to inch across the metallic table—Northern Virginia would be awake in a couple hours. I slid into the empty bench. AJ fiddled with the latch of his keys' carabiner, his nervous tell. He liked this girl.

Abebe ordered a cup of coffee with a side of toast. AJ ordered biscuits and gravy.

"Hon, what can I get you?" Our waitress smiled under a pile of curly hair. Just an empty skull in a wig. Her nametag, ironed onto a white button-up shirt, read HARRIET. After I ordered a large stack of pancakes, she stuck her mouth to the cop's ear and pointed back at us. A tall skinny kid with cheeks full of pimples served the rest of our meal.

Unable to bear the long flirting stares across the table, I kept darting my eyes away, only to catch the cop's glare. Half way through our meal, he pointed two fingers at me then back at his triangle eyes.

"That guard is freaking me out," I whispered.

Abebe clicked her tongue and leaned in close so a table of truck drivers next to us couldn't hear. "Why they need security? We're in fucking Virginia."

"Bad shit can happen anywhere," AJ said.

"You don't know nothin'."

"I know I can buy a quarter ounce in the parking lot." He was putting it on thick.

"That all?"

"I know it feels good," I interjected. I caught the brown of AJ's eyes, and darted my own away.

"White boys saying shit like that after smoking until they puke is the reason I live here," Abebe said, standing up and sliding on her parka. "I should go." She left half her food untouched, and didn't leave any money on the table.

"Good work," AJ said pelting his keys at me. They stabbed at my collarbone. "Can't keep your head down, can you?"

"Whatever," I whispered.

The waiter cleared our dishes. The ringed condensation from our glasses soaked through the bill. The cost of our meal was just under twenty dollars.

"So about that," AJ said. "That girl got my last bit of scratch." He rubbed the stubble on his jaw line. Screw this. No way was I paying for AJ's flirt session.

Abebe's hazy headlights flashed on in the flooded parking lot. My payback plan came to me in an instant. I palmed AJ's keys.

"Fuck!" I stood quickly and patted down my back pocket. "I left my wallet in her car," I lied.

It felt good to leave AJ there moneyless and alone, so good I didn't even avert my eyes when I passed the cop by the front door. I nodded at him and said, "Have a good one."

Outside, I ran around to the glass window by our booth and slammed my wallet against it. AJ jerked up. He looked at the wallet then into my eyes, and I mouthed *Fuck you*. He waved for me to come back in and I shook my head. The rain ran down my face. I backed away from the window and breathed in the wet air. I would drive around for thirty minutes, maybe an hour. I would come back. I would pay the bill. I just wanted to give him a little scare.

I never thought he'd chase after me. He crawled into the backseat, hands over his head, ducking and yelling "Go! GO! GO!" and "Fuck you!" and, "You knew I couldn't pay!"

My head was still clouded from the weed so I didn't think, I just did. I followed my body's orders. Before I knew it, the air bags exploded and we were wrapped around a parked sedan.

It felt like I had been out for hours, but it couldn't have been that long. I opened my eyes to a blinding light. A ringing in my ears subsided, and I heard boots from somewhere back and to my left, followed by radio static. Streaks of sunrise softened and came into focus through cracks in the windshield.

It wasn't raining anymore.

The inside of my right cheek burned and I tasted blood, then a hand was on my shoulder and someone dragged me out of the car and toward a cruiser parked near the IHOP entrance. I was adrift, glass sparkling on black cement, my neck sore from whiplash.

Later, I would learn the the cop claimed self defense. He thought I was trying to run him down. If you ask me, that fucker had time to move out of the way. He fired six rounds at us over unpaid pancakes. My face throbbed, my tongue hurt, and I was spread out over the hood of a police cruiser.

"Looks like you're fucked, son," a stubby hand slammed the bag of weed onto the hood of the cruiser.

"Don't you have to give me medical attention or something first?" I asked.

The cop held a thigh between my legs and I felt the jab of his belt.

"How about the grass, son?"

"Not mine."

"Bullshit. We found it in your Jeep."

"Not my car, check the plate."

"Uh huh." He put handcuffs on me and lifted me up by the arms.

The lot was now wrapped tight with tape. An ambulance spun light behind the crumpled Jeep.

"Where's AJ?"

"That the other guy?"

"Where is he?"

"Yup, son—you're fucked," the cop said as he pushed me down into the cruiser's backseat.

That's when I saw the body bag on a silver gurney.

SELFLESSLY, WITH PLEASURE

Purchasing the strap-on was all right, but expecting him to take it up the ass was much too much.

Charlotte, his wife of twelve years, had crossed the line, though why a woman in a straight, monogamous marriage would purchase a strap-on and expect to do anything other than put it in her husband's ass is anyone's guess. If only he had come clean and told her his feelings the moment she reached into the paper shopping bag and produced the strap-on while smiling that schoolgirl grin of hers, the one he swore he hadn't seen since grade school. It felt like it had been that long. If only he had admitted to her that all he wanted was to see her wear the strap-on and nothing more. He knew Charlotte was the kind of woman who would don it selflessly and with pleasure, so why he kept this secret is also anyone's guess. Perhaps he didn't even realize that this was something he wanted until just then.

From that day forward, he would often think about the strap-on. What its pink tip might look like poking out of Charlotte's bath robe while she did the dishes, or pushed a vacuum, or crawled on all fours to retrieve one of his stray New Balance sneakers from under the living room sofa.

Charlotte playfully tapped the dildo against his bottom lip. "Come on, don't get all sour," she said. He thought for a moment that he might lick the tip, but instead he took it from her left hand. He pointed it at her and said, "You are so greedy," before tossing it in the trash.

NOW THAT ALL DANGER IS AVERTED

The plan is to wander down the bright grocery store aisles and pretend to be strangers. It was John's idea. He said it would, how did he say it? "Spark something new"?

Olive will meet her husband by the frozen vegetables, or at the rows of canned soup, or in the Asian foods section and John will accidentally on purpose grab the same bag of carrots as her, or Olive will bump her shopping cart gently into his leg. They will both act as if they have never met each other before and it won't change anything.

There are other rules, but Olive cannot remember them. She cannot remember them because the whole thing is bullshit. Still, here she is after work, pulling into the parking lot of Harris Teeter. She slips a tiny little one hitter from her purse and packs it. Not the best idea in the world, but the only way.

When she is high, Olive has a beautiful lemon wedge smile, but she is not smiling as she gets out of the car, and weaves through the busy parking lot. Her lips are a single straight line in the middle of her wild face. The heel of one of her ballet flats slips off and she does not stop to fix it until she makes it to the shopping carts. She hates her stupid, stupid, business casual shoes and business casual slacks and business causal blouse. She throws her purse in the small basket and pulls out a shopping list. Olive has decided she wants to buy coconut popsicles. She scribbles "popsicles" on the piece of paper just below "fat-free yogurt," which is written in John's messy cursive. She then crosses out "fat-free."

After she puts seventy-eight dollars on her debit card, after she climbs back into her shitty Honda, putting the groceries in the passenger seat because she can't even bring herself to look in the back, after she barely makes it through a yellow light, she remembers John. That little shithead. That stupid freaking asshole. He didn't even show up. Well, screw John, she thinks as she pulls into the driveway of their small two story house. "I hate you," Olive says out loud when she yanks up on the parking break. *I hate you. I hate you. I hate you. I hate you, I hate you, I hate you, I hate you. I hate you. I hate you. I hate you. I hate you. I hate you.* Olive throws her hands onto the steering wheel. It was John's idea in the first place so she doesn't even know why she is so mad. Even though she is already stoned, Olive pulls out her tiny one hitter and packs it again.

John sits at a long wooden table in what is supposed to be their dining room but has, since building the nursery, turned into his office. He does not look up from his laptop when Olive opens the front door. He does not even say hello. He does stop typing to take a swig of the craft IPA he has just opened. He does place the bottle back on the table without using a coaster. He does look far too content as he slaps the space bar down entirely too loud as if he is so proud of every word. If John were to quit for just a moment, if he were to just look up over the edge of the computer screen, he would see his wife struggling with three grocery bags in each hand. He would see her drop them right there on the hardwood floor of their entranceway and stare him down with her dainty arms crossed over her flat chest. He would see her climb the stairs without even closing the front door. But he does not. He is not even aware of her presence.

Upstairs Olive pauses just outside the nursery. She pushes her knobby ear to the flat door, closes her eyes and imagines her baby's cries. For a moment she can even hear a high-pitched shriek, but when Olive opens her eyes the sound is gone.

*

Ten months ago Olive and John were painting the nursery walls custard because neither of them could stand the thought of having a pink room when John asked, "Have you ever wondered which of your parents would die first?"

Olive pushed the roller higher up the wall, and the bottom of her white, paint-speckled t-shirt rose to reveal her small belly.

"Like for the baby's sake, which one of us do you think should die first?"

"I don't know, J. Why are you asking me this?"

"Because, I always thought it'd be better if my dad died first, you know?"

"Why?" Olive asked.

"Because I think my mom would be less sad being alone."

"That's true."

"So who do you think would be more sad?" John asked.

"I don't know," Olive said. "Me, I guess."

They never stopped and considered other alternatives.

By the time John looks up from his laptop it is 10 p.m. and the coconut popsicles have melted inside their plastic sleeves. The grocery bags look like deflated balloons. What is wrong with her? Why can't she close the door, or put the groceries away or even say hello like a fucking normal person? It is not until he takes the tub of yogurt out of the bag, the not-even-half-fat yogurt, that he remembers.

When he crawls into bed wearing only his boxers, and he puts his knees up against the back of her knees, and wraps his free arm around her and says he is sorry, "I forgot," Olive inches further away from him.

"Are you mad?"

Olive rolls onto her back and shakes her head. "I didn't want to do it in the first place."

The ceiling fan is on high and the chain makes a faint clicking noise against the light fixture. After a long pause Olive says, "I want you to move your office into the nursery," before rolling back onto her side. She is as close to the edge of the bed as possible without falling off.

"I love you," John says.

Olive does not allow herself to hear it.

It used to be there in the quiet, everyday moments. When John spilled coffee, or pushed a strand of hair out of her eyes, or did the dishes, or said she looked beautiful. When they danced to Fleetwood Mac on the record player, or held hands in dark movie theaters, or ordered the same thing at restaurants. When they said it out loud for the first time, or had sex, or got drunk. When the little plastic stick turned to a pink plus sign, and five hours later John asked, "What if we keep it?"

But none of that compared.

It happened in that short period when they weren't

yet exhausted all the time, when they were both still excited about being parents. They both tiptoed into the baby's room—both of them—together, lifting their girl from her soft spot.

John's small, tan belly supported the weight of her in his right arm. His skinny hand cradled her head. He rocked back and forth from one foot to the next, his bare ass dancing in the dark. Then he sang. He sang long and deep, and it sounded like the soundtrack to a slowly burning fire. He sang and their girl's eyes were wide and green, and closing. He sang Baby Girl to sleep and Olive knew: this is what love sounds like.

Now she cannot hear it at all. Not even the slightest whisper.

Olive works in a gray cubicle in Farragut Square with a bunch of recent college graduates who care too much about their menial jobs. At thirty-two she is the oldest employee in the research department where her sole task is to update stupid press listings so stupid PR companies can spam stupid journalists. Her morning routine is as follows: roll out of bed at 7 a.m., rummage through the laundry hamper for the least wrinkled, least stupid business casual clothes she can find, do not eat breakfast, do not wake John. Drive to Metro station, pack tiny one hitter, ride Metro, arrive to work high and thirty minutes late. Pour sludgy coffee into Einstein mug, pretend to do work.

This morning Olive wonders how much longer she can continue being a bad worker. She wonders if management knows she is taking advantage of their sympathy. She wonders when all these barely-adults will stop looking at her like she is a mangy, lost dog.

At 10 a.m., right when Olive is about to start working, right when she is about to pick up the phone and call the *New York Times'* science desk to ask who covers alternative energy, James taps her on the shoulder. He is the token office gay. He wears polo shirts that are too tight and pants that hang too low on his hips. He is the only one that doesn't look at Olive like she has some sort of terminal illness.

"Cigarette?" James asks running a hand through his thick oily hair.

Olive nods.

In the park across the street Olive gives James fifty dollars, and James slips an eighth into her purse. He sucks the end of a cigarette. She packs her tiny one hitter. They do not talk. James knows better than to ask how she is doing.

Olive does not call the *New York Times* until an hour before she leaves work. Of course no one in particular exclusively covers alternative energy.

John is sitting at the long dining room table, the blue glow of his laptop reflecting off his tulip face and short blond hair. He does not look up when Olive opens the door. She stands in the entranceway staring at him, at his cleft chin, at his beady eyes, at the way his brow furrows when he takes a sip of his IPA. She is so, so angry. He can't do one simple thing? He can't just clean out the fucking nursery?

Olive stands there for almost five minutes before dropping her purse on the hardwood floor and stumbling upstairs without closing the front door again. Every stair she climbs she mutters, "I hate you." *I hate you, I hate you, I hate you. I hate you. I hate you. I hate you. I hate you. I hate you, I hate you, I hate you.*

Upstairs Olive closes her eyes and puts her ear to the nursery door. This time all she can hear is her own imagined voice whispering back, *I hate you, too.* Olive pounds against the door, her cheeks flushing red as she shakes her head furiously side to side. With every blow she thinks: *I don't care, I don't care, I don't care, I don't care. I don't care. I don't care. I don't care. I don't care, I don't care, I don't care. I don't care. I don't care. I don't care. I don't fucking care.*

When she finally stops, John's voice calls up to her, "Honey, is everything ok?"

"I'm fine," Olive yells back.

Their baby girl had no name. John subscribed to the thinking that they should get to know their child before giving her a title. For the two months she slept in the tiny crib on the second floor of their house, they simply just called her Baby Girl. This is the name used on the death certificate.

*

In the morning, Olive follows her normal routine. She digs out her stupid work casual clothes from the laundry hamper. She does not wake John. She does not eat breakfast. She packs the tiny one hitter. She rides the Metro. She arrives to work high and thirty minutes late. Before she can make it to the break room to pour a cup of coffee, before she can even drop her bag off at her grey cubicle, Olive's supervisor, Carl, calls her into his office. Down at the end of the hall James pops his head out from the top of his thin cubicle wall and gives her that worried, sympathetic look like the rest of these stupid, mindless drones before darting his glance away.

She doesn't look into Carl's eyes when she sits in the hard office chair across from his desk. She couldn't even if she wanted to. The light coming through the window behind Carl is so bright he is cast entirely in dark silhouette, and her eyes begin to water.

"I know you've been having a hard time," Carl says.

He passes her a box of tissues, but she doesn't take them. Olive wipes her eyes with the back of her hand. No, she is not crying. It is just the stupid bright light coming through the window. *Do not cry, do not cry, do not cry.*

"But you see," Carl says. "It has been three months and we're in the middle of a recession. We have to let you go."

"I understand," Olive says.

Carl gives her a small cardboard box to pack her things and Olive leaves the building without saying goodbye to anyone, not even James, or cleaning out her cube. As she rides the elevator down five flights, hugging the empty box to her chest, she remembers leaving at least three dirty, moldy Tupperware containers in the bottom drawer of her desk and she smiles.

The grass tastes like stale potpourri. The only splash of color on the front facade of her small house comes from the custard curtains still hanging in the unrecognizable window. Olive grabs the empty box in the passenger seat.

John is not at home, but his laptop is still there on the dining room table next to at least half a dozen mostly empty bottles of beer, and a plate with a quarter of an uneaten grilled cheese sandwich. Olive starts throwing John's papers and pencils and books into the box. She even puts the bottles sideways on top of all his shit and does not care if the small remnants of beer left in the bottoms spill onto his things. She lays the plate on top of the bottles and carries the box upstairs. Olive puts her ear to the nursery door again, and closes her eyes. This time she hears nothing. She places the box on the soft, white carpet in front of the door.

Then Olive goes and lies down in her bedroom, but the clinking of the chain against the light fixture of the ceiling fan drives her so crazy she rips her alarm clock from the wall socket and throws it. The clock hits and the glass shatters down onto the floral bedspread but the fan keeps spinning, the chain now tinging against the bare tungsten light bulb. "Fuck you," Olive screams. *Fuck you, fuck you, fuck you!*

In those two months Olive had developed new routines. She checked warmth of milk on wrist. She counted her daughter's daily bowel movements. She hardly slept. She never smoked. Milk, shit, sleep, baby. Milk, lactate, baby. She never had a lapse of judgement. Sleep, baby. Shit, baby. Milk for baby.

Never say never.

"Not okay, Olive," John says slamming the box of papers and books and beer bottles onto their bed. The box bounces an inch off the mattress and the plate with the grilled cheese slides off, landing face down on the white carpet in front of Olive's bare feet. She is sitting with her elbows on her knees and back against the wall. She doesn't say anything as he paces back and forth in the room and yells.

"You can't keep doing this to me," he says. "I can't stand you acting like a passive-aggressive little girl."

He kneels down in front of her, and cups her face in his hands. Her cheeks are red and chapped from crying. "Olive. Why are you doing this?"

She tries to say she doesn't know. She tries to say she is sorry. She tries to at least lean forward and hug him, but she can't. She grabs his hands and removes them from her face, and then crosses her arms.

"Fine," John says. "Fine. Fine. Fine. Fine. Fine."

He walks out of the room and down the hall and goes into the nursery.

"Is this what you want?" He emerges from the nursery with a children's book clutched in his hand, and he throws it down the stairs. He goes back for an armful of stuffed animals, and throws those too. Olive is on her feet now and coming down the hallway. Next is the purple umbrella stroller. Olive hears it slide down the stairs like a wooden spoon on a washboard.

"Stop it," Olive yells. She grabs John's wrists as he turns from the stairwell back towards the nursery. "Stop it."

John does not fight her grasp. He does not yell back. He doesn't say anything as his arms go limp and Olive is left there, just outside the nursery door only inches apart from him but without any idea of how to close such a distance.

"I just—" Olive pauses. "I can't have her things in this house any more."

"Okay," John says to the floor. He can't even look her in the eye. "I just thought, maybe someday you would come around and want another."

"I don't," Olive says. "Can you live with that?"

*

The plan is to pretend to be strangers. They wander the bright grocery store aisles in search of something new. Olive wears freshly laundered jeans and a white t-shirt. She is examining the oranges when a hand reaches for the exact same one. His warm fingers brush over the back of her hand and Olive pulls hers away.

AT BAT

Number 28 slams the butt of his bat to the ground and the 24-ounce weight slides off. From under his red batting helmet the right fielder is all shaggy, shoulder-length locks and facial hair. A fan in centerfield waves a sign with his nickname THE BEARD printed in big block letters. This, right here, is what Number 28 has been dreaming of every night since he can remember. Game four of the National League Division Series is tied one to one in the bottom of the ninth. He is the first guy up. The bullpen's arms are dead so he can' t let this game slip away into extra innings. Lose and his teammates back there leaning against the dugout railing, hope still in their eyes, pack up their bags and fly home to Nevada or Ohio or wherever it is they live in the off-season, and they don't come back until spring training. Some of them might never come back.

Number 28 taps the bat on the inside of each cleat and adjusts the Velcro of his white batting gloves. He is more careful with the left hand. Though his doctors have said the break is fully healed, his wrist hasn't felt the same since the diving catch he made four months ago that put him on the bench for half the season. He puts a hand on the top of his helmet before digging into the batter's box. He stares down the Pitcher, a tall hook of a righty with a 98 m.p.h. fastball. When he pulls the bat back behind his right ear, the roar of all 44,000 fans in attendance fades away. He cannot hear a thing. All Number 28 has to do is get on base. A walk, a single to left or a big knock over the centerfield wall, it does not matter. Baseball is a simple game. See the ball. Hit the ball. Become a hero.

Number 28 eyes two screaming fastballs right into the catcher's mitt and already it is an 0-2 count. The pitch speed, 94 m.p.h., flashes on the jumbo scoreboard out in right field.

Coco cannot believe it. She turns to her husband Robbie, puts her left hand over her wrinkled eyes and says, "I can't watch—I might throw up," not because she has had too much to drink, but because she is nervous. She cares too much. They are standing in front of their seats in Section

217, one level up, between first and home plate. They are both decked out in the home team's gear, red sweatshirts and baseball caps with curly Ws on the front. Empty plastic cups that used to contain beer are littered at their feet. They each have an earbud in one ear, the long white cords coming together around a small radio in their clasped hands. Though it is a crisp October evening, the tips of Robbie's fingers feel sweaty between Coco's knuckles.

Coco has watched every home game with her husband from these seats since the ballpark opened in 2008 while listening to the game play by play on 106.7 FM. She has endured horrible seasons, but 2009 when her beloved team lost 108 games, and 2010 when they lost 93 more, are distant memories. Now she feels like a winner. This is the playoffs. After marriage, and kids, and grandkids, after retirement and their dream trip to Dubrovnik, this is what she has been hoping for. It is the last of her major life events. Something to retell at family dinners. Remember the World Series of 2012?

Well, they've got to get there first.

The fans around them start chanting Beard! Beard! Beard! It is a far cry from the hate fans spewed just last year when Number 28 arrived in the District and went through a dismal batting slump. On more than one occasion both Coco and Robbie had screamed a profanity or two down at the field when Number 28 struck out looking. Now the fans are so loud Coco can barely hear Robbie when he moves her hand from her face and says, "It's okay. The Rookie is up next."

Coco rolls her eyes at the prospect. This is not a time for sarcasm.

Number 28 sits on pitch number three, a 81 m.p.h. curveball that misses down and away, slipping from the catcher's mitt and bouncing against the backstop with a thud. He spits on another junk pitch for ball two. He steps out of the box, takes in a deep breath and adjusts the Velcro of his batting gloves again. He takes two big practice swings before stepping back in. Okay, Righty. You're missing with that curve, aren't ya? I'm gettin' straight heat. He taps home plate with the end of his bat and then swings it back. The Pitcher cocks his leg up, hiding the red bird printed on his jersey, and then lunges forward, unleashing a fastball on the inside, at Number 28's fists. He swings and the ball ricochets off the inner half of his bat, a twinge of pain radiating in his left wrist as the ball loops back into the crowd behind home plate.

Number 28 steps out of the box.

"You got this," yells the 19-year-old Rookie in the on-deck circle as he takes a practice swing. Though the sun has long since set behind the stadium on the third base side The Rookie is still wearing red contacts to fight off glare. So far in the playoffs he is 1 for 18. He is due for a hit, but nerves have clearly gotten the better of him. Behind The

Rookie in the hole is the third baseman. He is the face of the franchise, the only starting player that has been with the team since their first season in the District. Franchise has a boyish charm, a round face and goofy eyes but lately this twenty-six year old star has has begun to show his age, needing three cortisone shots in his right shoulder over the course of the season, and regularly missing routine throws from third to first.

Number 28 nods at The Rookie, and eyes Franchise who is rubbing the shoulder of his throwing arm. It's all an awful lot of pressure. 28 adjusts the Velcro of his batting gloves. 28 puts a hand on top of his helmet when he digs in. He reminds himself to just get on base. He remembers how simple it is.

Number 28 pops up a pitch that lands in the dug-out just four feet to the right of Franchise. The Bench Coach puts a cleat up onto the top step of the dugout and says, "This is getting interesting," before spitting used tobacco on the cement floor. The whole bench begins to chatter, recalling a game in Miami from the regular season. After waiting out a two-hour rain delay where they were down by one run, Number 28 came up to the plate in the ninth. He fouled off at least five pitches before knocking a game tying solo shot into the Fish's bullpen.

"He has a knack for doing it, doesn't he?" Coach says just as Number 28 barely gets a piece of a low breaking ball.

*

Number 28 looks up at the pitch count on the jumbotron. Ten pitches? Is that right? The pitcher runs his fingers along the bill of his baseball cap then stares into home plate for the catcher's call. Number 28 points the end of his bat to the visitor's bullpen then pulls it back behind his right ear where it circles in anticipation for the next pitch. Okay, Righty, I can foul these suckers off all night long. The ball is hurled from the pitcher's mound, a fastball down the middle. Number 28 begins to swing, but something's not right. The ball begins to drop, and just at the last second 28 catches a flash of the red stitches rotating downward. He holds up his swing, and the 79 m.p.h. breaking ball hooks down and away, crossing the plate just on the outside corner and landing in the catcher's mitt with a thwack. Number 28 knows instantly that the call could go either way. If it's a ball he's still alive; strike and it's up to The Rookie and Franchise to win this game. He waits for a called strike that never comes, and holds his breath as the visiting team appeals to the first base ump whose arms spread wide for the call.

He did not swing.

Number 28 exhales when he steps out of the box. He is still alive. For the first time since walking up to the plate he is aware of the roar of the stadium, fans waiting to explode, waiting for the win. He adjusts his gloves for what feels like the hundredth time.

*

"What if we don't win?" Coco asks.

"Then we go home," Robbie says, "And we come back next year."

"But what if we suck next year?"

"We will not suck. And anyway, how about a little optimism. We are going to win this game," Robbie says as Number 28 fouls off the twelfth pitch. The ball travels fifty feet in the air, and is almost eye level with the press box where the radio play-by-play broadcasters are calling the game.

"Remember the at-bat after the rain delay Dave?" Charlie asks into the microphone. He has a round nose and a receding hairline, and his eyes are set entirely too far apart.

"I do," Dave says.

"Remember what happened culminating that at-bat?"

"I do."

"Wouldn't that be nice?" Charlie asks.

"I hope you're The Summoner."

"I hope I can steal a little summoning from you, Dave."

The Pitcher throws his thirteenth pitch, a 96 m.p.h. mistake. A ball that fast takes only a few fractions of a second to travel the sixty feet, six inches from the rubber of the pitcher's mound to home plate. The batter has even less time to decide if it is a pitch worth swinging at. This pitch is a no-brainer right down the middle of the plate. The knock of the wooden bat on the ball is unmistakable, like the sound of a cork from a champagne bottle; that kind of pop only means one thing. The moment the ball explodes off Number 28's bat Charlie and Dave are on their feet. The ball flies over the infield, and at sixty feet in the air glimpses the white dome of the Capital Building a mile beyond the outfield.

"The ball is going, going—" and before Charlie finishes the sentence, the ear buds fall from Coco's ear. She waves both hands in the air, and the small radio falls to the ground and lands in an empty beer cup. Number 28 is already at first base pointing at Franchise, who is leading the charge out of the dugout, when the ball lands in the visitor's bullpen some 406 feet from home plate. Right now it does not matter what happens tomorrow, or the next day, or even if they make it to the pennant. Tonight Number 28 did his job.

Baseball is a simple game.

ACKNOWLEDGMENTS

Versions of these stories have appeared elsewhere:

"How Tommy Soto Breaks Your Heart" — *Annalemma*

"Felicia Sassafras Is Fiction" — Yes Press Books

"Raz-Jan" — *Hair Trigger*

"At Bat" — *Hobart*

"Over Shell Drive" — *The Spoiler's Hand*

Many thanks to the Curbside team—Victor Giron, Naomi Huffman, Jacob Knabb, and Ben Tanzer; my editor, Peter Jurmu, for his patient eyes and ears; Nick Marshall for his beautiful photograph and Alban Fischer for designing the shit out of this book; Shannon Murphy for being a great reader and a better friend; and to my teachers, Joe Meno and Babak Elahi, for their support and good counsel. Lastly, I'm especially grateful to my parents for raising me well and with love.

SUSAN HOPE LANIER earned an MFA in creative writing from Columbia College in 2012 and currently lives, writes, and photographs in Chicago, Illinois.

DOES NOT LOVE
A novel by James Tadd Adcox

"...Adcox is a writer who knows how to make the reader believe the impossible, in his capable hands, is always possible, and the ordinary, in his elegant words, is truly extraordinary."

—Roxane Gay, author of *Bad Feminist* and *An Untamed State*

Set in an archly comedic alternate reality version of Indianapolis that is completely overrun by Big Pharma, James Tadd Adcox's debut novel chronicles Robert and Viola's attempts to overcome loss through the miracles of modern pharmaceuticals. Viola falls out of love following her body's third "spontaneous abortion," while her husband Robert becomes enmeshed in an elaborate conspiracy designed to look like a drug study.

LET GO AND GO ON AND ON
A novel by Tim Kinsella

"I give Kinsella a five thousand star review for launching me deep into an alternate universe somewhere between fiction of the most intimate and biography of the most compelling. It's like...a pitch-perfect fine flowing bellow, the sound of celestial molasses." **—Devendra Banhart**

Let Go and Go On and On is the story of obscure actress Laurie Bird. Told in a second-person narrative, blurring what little is known of her actual biography with her roles as a drifter in *Two Lane Blacktop*, a champion's wife in *Cockfighter*, and an aging rock star's Hollywood girlfriend in *Annie Hall*, the story unravels in Bird's suicide at the age of 26. *Let Go and Go On and On* explores our endless fascination with the Hollywood machine and the weirdness that is celebrity culture.

CRAZY HORSE'S GIRLFRIEND
A novel by Erika T. Wurth

"Crazy Horse's Girlfriend *is gritty and tough and sad beyond measure; but is also contains startling, heartfelt moments of hope and love. In my opinion, a writer can't do much better than that.*" —**Donald Ray Pollock,** author of *Knockemstiff* and *Donnybrook*

Margaritte is a sharp-tongued, drug-dealing, sixteen-year-old Native American floundering in a Colorado town crippled by poverty, unemployment, and drug abuse. She hates the burnout, futureless kids surrounding her and dreams that she and her unreliable new boyfriend can move far beyond the bright lights of Denver that float on the horizon before the daily suffocation of teen pregnancy eats her alive.

THE OLD NEIGHBORHOOD
A novel by Bill Hillmann

"*A raucous but soulful account of growing up on the mean streets of Chicago, and the choices kids are forced to make on a daily basis. This cool, incendiary rites of passage novel is the real deal.*"

—**Irvine Welsh,** author of *Trainspotting*

The Old Neighborhood is the story of teenager Joe Walsh, the youngest in a large, mixed-race family living in Chicago. After Joe witnesses his older brother commit a gangland murder, his friends and family drag him down into a pit of violence that reaches a bloody impasse when his elder sister begins dating a rival gang member. The Old Neighborhood is both a brutal tale of growing up tough in a mean city, and a beautiful harkening to the heartbreak of youth.